CLOWN ALLEY

Book One

The Adventures of Fiveish the Clown

Text Copyright 2017 by Frank Michael Adams
ISBN-13: 978-1-521468579

Illustrations Copyright 2017 by Sonnaz

Website: www.clownalleybooks.com
Email: contact@clownalleybooks.com

CLOWN ALLEY
Book One

THE ADVENTURES OF FIVEISH THE CLOWN

By
FRANK MICHAEL ADAMS
Illustrations by Sonnaz

Dedication

To Mark Lundy, friend, Gymnastic Coach and
Pac-10 Ring Champion; he will be remembered as an
inspiration to the entire S.S.U. Gymnastics Team.

To Fred Churchack, acting and physical comedy
coach who's mastery of theater from different ages,
cultures and styles, have inspired many
and guided me towards the magical link
where tumbling meets comedy.

Contents

CLOWN ALLEY
Book One

The Adventures of Fiveish the Clown

THERE ONCE WAS a clown named Fiveish. He was a clever clown, the talk of the town. Children and their parents loved the little fellow. He could warm the heart of even the biggest bully. But then one day...

Chapter One
Enter the Man

FIVEISH STEPPED OUT from the yellow taxi. The driver quickly rolled down his window, "Hey Bub, you owe me five dollars."

Looking at his distorted reflection in the window, Fiveish fixed his black bowtie then flicked the cash at the driver hitting him square in the forehead then walked away.

"Bozo!" yelled the cab driver, "What's the matter with you?"

Fiveish crossed the street then sprung up the steps of the performance hall. Turning around before entering, he looked out at the bustling traffic and crowds of people. He smiled then lifted his arms into the air as if they were his wings.

"I have arrived," he said like a king stepping out from his chariot.

Taking a deep breath, filling his lungs with fresh smoggy air, he bent over and coughed repeatedly. Smoothing out his black suit, he quickly entered into the lobby. Jogging through the theater, avoiding conversation with employees or friendly well-wishers, he hopped up onto the stage going directly to his changing room. On his way, he passed the Ringmaster who turned and followed him with his gaze.

~⁀⁓

IT WAS GOING to be a special performance. It was special because the children that would watch the show were orphans. Some had no memories of their parents. Some only recently lost them and were very sad. These were children who needed some happiness. And that is what Fiveish the Clown was there to do, Fiveish the Clown but not Fiveish the Man.

The Ringmaster with his red tailcoat and gray top hat marched onto the stage.

"And now!" he belted out with a powerful voice that thundered throughout the auditorium, "children of all ages, what you have all been waiting for, that silly slouch, that gallant goof, your friend and mine, Fiveish the Clown!"

The clown sprinted on stage balancing a ladder on top of his head. In one hand was a bucket, in the other a paintbrush. He ran in a circle around the stage.

The ladder teetered to the left then tottered to the right. It was on the verge of falling with every tilt. Then his paint pants fell down, slipping below his knees.

The baggy pants sank all the way to his ankles, tangling them up. The clown fell forward with the ladder, crashing upside down on the rungs.

Being stuck upside down caused his pants to fall downside up and back to normal.

There was a burst of laughter.

Untangling himself, the clown put the paint bucket down onto the floor, dipped the paintbrush into it, climbed the ladder then reached up to paint the ceiling. It was too high. He climbed another rung. He stretched his arms up as high as he could then fell over the top of the ladder, flipping like a tossed rag, landing into the paint bucket, seat first.

"Oof!"

The children laughed out loud.

He tried to get out but his bottom was wedged in. He rocked back and forth until he rolled over onto his hands and knees.

"Help!" he yelled, with the bucket on top like a turtle shell.

The Ringmaster hurried on stage, grabbed the bucket and pulled but it wouldn't come off. Then with a kick the clown fell off the stage right into the orchestra.

Violins flew into the air; symbols rolled every which way; a clarinet fell into a tuba and got jammed in.

The Ringmaster waved to the Stagehand who quickly joined him. They jumped down then lifted the bucket back onto the stage with the sad clowns rear end still stuck in it, his feet dangling listlessly below.

The audience howled with laughter.

A crowbar was brought in. They pried, tweaked and yanked it. It was the yank that did it. The bucket flew off with a pop. The ringmaster and the stagehand went flying with a crash and a bang.

The clown stood, looked at the audience then

rubbed his Gluteus Maximus, in other words his posterior and in other words his clown behind.

"Oooo! That hurt," he said.

He took a step with his big clown shoe… right back into the paint bucket.

He looked at the audience.

"Ahhh!" he whimpered.

He lifted his foot into the air; the bucket came up with it. It was stuck like glue. He shook it to no avail. He ran in a circle while the bucket went "clank, clank, clank." Giving up, he looked at the audience.

"Waaa!" he cried.

The children laughed and laughed.

The ringmaster rushed back on stage.

"Does anyone want to help Fiveish get his foot unstuck?"

Over a hundred hands shot up, and dozens of children yelled, "Pick me! Pick me!"

A little girl was brought up on stage as a volunteer.

Sitting on the floor, the clown lifted the bucket then pointed it towards the girl. She tried to pull it off his clown shoe but ended up pulling him across the stage on his clown rear end.

This time the clown held onto the ladder. She pulled and she tugged as Fiveish slid across the floor with the ladder trailing behind. The Ringmaster, along with the Stagehand ran then jumped onto the ladder.

Finally, "snap!" the bucket shot off. But Fiveish's big clown shoe was covered in paint.

Sliding on the paint the poor clown tumbled over a chair, slipped on his chest across the stage then crashed into a grand piano, which fell on top of him. The musical instrument fell apart around him with an explosion of dust.

He looked at the audience then smiled.

The laughter was so loud that people walking by outside the theater could hear it.

"Give her a big round of applause!" yelled the Ringmaster.

The children clapped for the little girl as she was escorted back to her seat.

Later, after the curtain closed at the end of the show, the clown walked down the hall towards his dressing room.

"Great job Fiveish," said the producer, "the kids loved you."

"Thank you," he said.

The clown was very happy with the performance. He was tired but felt light as if he were floating.

"Awesome job Fiveish!" said the curtain man.

"Thanks, I appreciate it," said the humble little clown.

He often felt this way after making so many children and adults happy.

"You made me laugh so hard," said the light technician, "that I had to run to the bathroom!"

"Thank you, thank you," said the clown, his heart flying with happiness.

He passed the Ringmaster who was leaning against the wall near the door of his changing room.

"Impressive show today clown," said the Ringmaster. "You've managed to make many unfortunates happy."

"Thank you sir," he said. "You're very kind."

"Oh no, quite the contrary," responded the Ringmaster, "It is you who is very kind. Try to remember that, won't you?"

"Yes sir," he said, as he stepped into his changing room.

The Ringmaster lifted his top hat then began tapping it with his fingers tips. His eye behind the glass monocle squinted as he smiled with an odd curl to his upper lip.

Closing the door behind him, the clown walked across the changing room then sat before his mirror. He turned on the switch and a circle of bulbs lit up around his reflection. He looked into the mirror. He had a very big smile on his sad clown face.

He grabbed his rubber nose then pulled. Slowly, the spirit gum stretched then gave way, the nose snapping off from his clown face.

He looked back into the mirror. He was no longer smiling.

Lifting the clown hat off his head, he threw it into the laundry bag.

His lips tightened. A frown formed on his face.

Dipping a sponge into a jar of makeup remover; he then wiped the grease paint across his face, causing it to streak. As he rubbed his face the makeup swirled into a sloppy rainbow of colors, black, white, red and blue. The more he did it, the more he looked like a nightmare image of a scary creature. He stopped for a moment to just stare at his reflection.

"Ooooooo!" he said like a ghost. "What's the matter kids am I scaring you?"

He smiled an unfriendly smile then twisted his lip, morphing his makeup into a freakish mask.

"You don't like the way I look?" he snarled to nobody.

The stage manager peaked in through the open door.

"Are you okay?" he asked. "I thought I heard moaning."

"Get out of here and close the door," he answered abruptly. "And don't bother me."

Wiping off the rest of his makeup, the clown looked into the mirror again but this time he was no longer the clown, he was the man.

He stood then began changing into his regular clothes, black suit with a black bowtie. He combed his hair then stepped into the hallway.

"I really liked your painter act Fiveish," said the prop woman with a smile.

"I do not need your words of appreciation," said Fiveish the Man, "and I do not want them. So please leave my presence forthwith."

The prop woman quickly lost her smile.

He made his way towards the lobby.

"Wow! You were…"

"Don't bother me!" he said to the set designer, not letting him finish his sentence. "Leave me alone! Mind your own business?"

The set designer stood silently for a moment trying to figure out what he said or did to make Fiveish so discourteous.

Gathering his pluck, the set designer rejoined, "You don't make sense. You're gentle and caring when you're on stage. Everyone loves you, and you seem to love everyone else."

With a smirk he replied, "You're talking about Fiveish the Clown. I am Fiveish the Man."

Chapter Two
Enter the Clown

ONE DAY WHILE reclining on his sofa at home, Fiveish received a phone call.

Picking up the receiver, he said, "Speak."

"Hey Fiveish, it's Sal," said the voice on the other side.

"Sal who?"

"Sal, Sal your talent agent you goofy goof!"

"Oh, its Salad Face Sal, my bum agent. What do you want now, more of my money?"

"Not this time clown face. But later you're going to owe me. I booked you for a good one this time. Thank me. Come on, thank me."

"I am not in the mood for the foolish talk of a fool. What do you want already?"

"You're booked to perform at the Mystique in five weeks!"

Shocked, Fiveish asked, "What did you say?"

"You heard me goofball," said Salad Face.

"You must be kidding!" said Fiveish.

Salad Face Sal remained silent.

"You're not kidding? This is wonderful; this is fantastic!"

"I knew you'd like that news," said Salad. "Just want to let you know though that this is going to be a big one. There will be television cameras and newspaper reporters."

"This is my big chance," yelled Fiveish. "I'm going to be rich! I'm going to be famous! I'll buy a boat, a castle!"

Fiveish paused.

"Wait a minute, wait a minute. How much are you skimming off the top, you salad faced sneak."

"Take it easy," said the Salad; "the usual twenty percent."

"You are still a thief," said Fiveish as he slammed down the phone.

THE CROWDED TRAIN sped across the Oakenstock Bridge. Wrinkling his nose at the unpleasant aroma that wafted past him, Fiveish's mind wandered to trivial thoughts.

"Is this a Subway or an L-train?" he thought to himself.

The train passed the Old Navy Shipyard then hit a sharp turn. An elderly woman bumped into him. She lost the grip on her bag of groceries. Fruits and vegetables scattered across the floor.

"What do you want? Get away!" said Fiveish sharply.

"I'm sorry to disturb you," she said, "but you look like a nice young man. The old arthritis is acting up. Could you help me with these?"

He didn't reply.

The elderly lady slowly bent to gather what had fallen. She winced in pain, holding her back.

With a wicked smile Fiveish watched the lady while mumbling to himself, "Overpass, underpass, Subway, L-train, la, la, la."

The train zoomed past the Wellcatch Oil Refinery. Smoke, rusted steel and brown water filled the horizon. The smell was terrible.

Leaving the refinery behind, the elevated train entered No Mans Land, the outskirts of town.

Abandoned apartments whizzed by with not a single occupied dwelling. Every window was either boarded or broken. There were endless rows of gray brick without tree or shrub, car or human. It was lifeless.

The words, grit and grime popped into his mind.

Then down below the tracks in the midst of No Mans Land, the curtain of a single unbroken window slipped open. A white face peered out; its eyes hidden by large round sunglasses. It seemed to follow the train as it bolted along the elevated track.

"Who would live in such a place?" he whispered, as the white face fell back into the distance.

The city skyline approached. The train stopped when it reached Down Town.

As soon as Fiveish stepped off the train a man

dressed in rags approached him. His shoes had holes in them and the heels were worn to the bottom.

"Mister, could you spare some change?" the ragged man asked. "I am sick and have no family to help me."

Fiveish the man stuck his hands out, palms up, in front of the man. A silver dollar rested in his left hand. He turned his hand's palms down while quickly closing them into a fist.

"Which hand," he asked? There was a mischievous smile on his face.

I want to inform the reader at this time that Fiveish the Clown was a world-class comic acrobat, not a magician. Generally clowns specialize in a single area of variety entertainment but are often a jack-of-all-trades in the other variety arts. For example: there are clowns who specialize in the unicycle, and most of their show is based on that. But they also practice juggling, face painting or teeter board though not as much.

So, even though Fiveish studied magic, he was no magician. But he did have just enough tricks to either bother people or make them feel foolish.

The ragged man looked from fist to fist. He needed to guess correctly because he hadn't eaten since the day before. His desperate eyes moved from left to right. Was the left fist just a little bigger than the right or was the right fist just a little bigger than the left? The poor man scratched his head.

"The left!" he cried.

Opening his hands, palms up, it was revealed to the poor man that they were empty.

street overhead, left a wind that echoed off the walls, morphing into ghostlike wales.

He began to relax.

In the distance, a glowing light filled the underground tunnel. Moving closer, he could hear the far away sound of circus music.

Then there it was, the entrance to Clown Alley.

Chapter Three
Clown Alley

THE ENTRANCE HAD a wooden archway over the top with exquisite carvings of theatrical masks etched into it. At the top of the arch were displayed the traditional masks of the happy face, sad face of theater throughout the ages. However, the happy face seemed just a little too happy, almost insane in fact. And the sad face seemed just a little too sad, almost tortured in fact.

Down the left side of the archway were carved the colorful masks of the Commedia Dell'arte, the Italian theatrical characters of the Renaissance. He touched the mask of Harlequin the acrobatic clown and then Pierrot the sad-faced clown. He laughed at the sad face, comparing it to his own as Fiveish the Clown. Some of the masks were freakish with big oversized foreheads, cheeks or chins.

"Faces one might see in a nightmare," he thought.

Along the right side were carved the hysterical, grotesque and often frightening masks of the ancient Japanese Kabuki Theater, with bright colors, wild eyes and long tongues sticking out. One mask painted red and yellow snarled with its gaping mouth and large fangs.

The circus music pumping into the tunnel pulled his attention away from the strange faces.

He stepped under the arch to the other side.

"Ah, that's more like it."

Fiveish had now officially entered Clown Alley. The world lit up with bright colors. He walked along a cobblestone street lined with fruit trees, flowers, and beautiful vines. The smell of popcorn and bubble gum was in the air. Children and adults were playing in a park. The sound of circus music was everywhere. There was laughter, happiness and sunshine.

"Sunshine? But I am underground, am I not?"

This kind of cheerful atmosphere made Fiveish the Man uncomfortable. For him, there was too much laughter and too many smiling faces.

"I have never seen this part of town before."

There were large carnival tents of all colors and designs on both sides of the cobblestone street. Strange looking entertainers with odd costumes stood by their entrances and watched Fiveish as he passed. Their faces looked far away and dreamy. They tried to wave Fiveish towards them.

"Come see what is inside," said one of them who looked like a gypsy. Her hair was black with golden streaks that almost reached to the ground. She opened the tent flap a little wider.

"Come and see, come and see," she said.

Fiveish wanted to. He wanted to go through that

tent flap. He wanted to see what was inside. In fact, he desperately wanted to. His curiosity was almost overwhelming, but he did not understand why. He became frightened. Acting as if he were ignoring her, he quickened his steps and walked on.

There was a breeze that caused the tents to beat in the wind. He looked up. Clouds moved quickly across the sky.

"Odd," he said. "It is daylight yet I can clearly see the stars."

In fact, the sky was full of stars, countless thousands, and shooting stars as well. The sky was blue but not like a blue he had ever seen before. It was the blue of glacial melt in a mountain valley; silver sparkles floated in it, moving all about.

He blinked his eyes.

"Where is that confounded Mystique Theater!" he said to himself.

There was a crowd up ahead. Children and adults were laughing and clapping.

He made his way through the crowd.

"Aha! A juggler. Oh, I just love jugglers."

He pushed his way into the opening in the middle of the circle.

The juggler performed in his colorful tights. Balls, rings, clubs and an open umbrella flew in hypnotic circles like Ptolemy's orbital spheres of the solar system. The colorful balls looked like planets speeding in their odd journey around the Sun.

Fiveish the man loved jugglers because if you

bump into them in mid jug, the balls, clubs, and rings would fly away bouncing in erratic trajectories, rolling under peoples legs, bouncing off spectators heads, falling into storm drains never to be found again, etc.

And that is exactly what he did. With a nasty smile, he walked right into the juggler then just kept on walking. Small giggly laughs escaped from his lips as he quickly walked away and disappeared into the crowd leaving the poor juggler with his ruined show to run after all his props that flew every which way.

On he walked.

"Ah, what a lovely day this is becoming," he said.

He passed a carousel blasting out calliope music. The children and adults had silly smiles or goofy laughs as they sat on their colorful horses spinning around the outer orb of the musical platform. One child looked as if he were holding on for dear life; the look of terror was apparent on his face. His hands clasped the bar in front of him so tightly that his fingers were turning white.

Fiveish was amused.

The spin it seemed was circling just a little too fast for the children. Their heads leaned far to the outside of the circling contraption due to centrifugal force, and their necks were straining due to that force.

"What a pain in the neck," he said with a naughty chuckle.

"Ah, what's this?"

A circus performer practiced his walk along a slack line tied between two plum trees. Rehearsing for an outdoor show scheduled for later that evening, he seemed to be struggling a bit for he was always on the verge of falling either to the left or to the right.

Fiveish's eyes lit up.

He nonchalantly walked towards the performer, while remaining slightly behind his peripheral vision, enough so as not to be seen. The slackline walker was just reaching the middle of the line, and his balance was just becoming stable when Fiveish the man put his hands on one of the plum trees. He vigorously pushed back and forth on the tree causing a rainstorm of ripe plums to fall onto the slack line and its bewildered performer.

The slackline walker began to wobble. His leg lifted high into the air to counterbalance, but then he fell in a tangled mess onto the loose line. He bounced and spun off the line to land in a heap in the grass.

He stood up brushing the dirt, grass and squashed fruit off his practice uniform. He looked for the mean culprit who did this to him. He saw a man walking away, but he was wearing a black suit with a bowtie.

He scratched his head then thought, "People with black suits and bowties don't pull mean pranks on circus acrobats."

The man was now gone anyway, already mixed in with the wandering spectators.

Fiveish had a lively spring to his step and could not help smiling at the wonderful joy he was experiencing today. He smelled the flowers and took in the sunshine and light breeze.

"Well, how about that!" he said. "There actually is a purpose for flowers after all. They smell absolutely magnificent! But, I won't tell the flower peddler about that, he-he, hoo-hoo."

He turned in a circle, taking in the odd spectacle.

"Clown Alley is really something. I never even knew that it existed. I must venture back here again. Now, where is that theater? It's getting late!"

He stopped at a food stand called, "Food, Food and more Food."

The lady behind the register asked, "What can I get you?"

"Corn Dog," he answered.

The cornmeal-dipped hot dog with a stick was placed into the deep fryer. It sizzled and popped in the hot oil.

"Can I get anything else for you?" she politely asked.

No answer from Fiveish the Man, there was just disturbing silence.

"Okay," thought the food preparer, "that's a rude one."

She handed him the Corndog. Fiveish quickly snatched it from her hand and took a bite.

"This Corndog is simply horrible!" he said. "It's terribly disgusting. Don't you taste your own food to make sure it's good? How can you serve this slop to your customers?"

"That's one dollar and fifty cents, sir," she replied coldly.

"I'll not pay for this unhealthy, dangerous even poisonous food!" he yelled, as he began walking away.

"I am calling the health department! I'll see my lawyer for this, you can be sure of that!"

When he was safely lost in the crowd, he said, "Mmm what a sumptuous corndog, so tasty and tender with just the right amount of crispiness. Must not eat too much though, don't' want to be heavy for the show."

He threw the corndog stick on the ground right next to a trashcan.

"Hey mister, that's littering," said a little boy holding his mother's hand.

"That wasn't very nice," said his mother. "You should pick it back up and toss it into the garbage can."

"Keep your business between your own two ears," said Fiveish the man.

"Ah the smell of popcorn and cotton candy," he sighed with pleasure. If only there were less noisy children with their nagging parents ruining it all."

"Welcome, welcome to one and all!" said a voice through a megaphone. "Step right up and take your seats for the next exciting show!"

"Oh goody!" said Fiveish. "There's another show starting."

He took a seat right in front of the outdoor stage. He was very excited. Other spectators meandered in and found seats.

A clown walked on stage. It was a white-faced clown, with big red lips, stars on its cheeks and a rainbow-colored clown wig. Its costume was huge and billowing with giant red buttons shaped like hearts.

Fiveish couldn't contain himself. He was shaking with happiness like a child.

"A clown!" he said to the lady at his left.

"A clown!" he said to the man at his right.

Both man and lady scooted a few inches away from him.

He was so loud with his enthusiasm that someone from behind yelled, "Shut up!"

The rainbow wig clown became distracted by all the commotion and forgot what to do.

"Hi everybody!" it eventually said. "Are you having a great time today?"

"Yes!" answered the crowd.

It reached into a small satchel then pulled out a balloon. Pointing to a little boy it said, "What would you like me to make?"

The little boy answered, "Addition number three hundred and twenty six of Super Stooge Comics!"

Rainbow wig blankly stared at the kid for a moment.

The audience cracked up at this.

Fiveish loved this kid. Of course, Fiveish the man really did not love anybody, but if he could, it would be that kid.

"Pick something else," it said, becoming flustered, "not a comic book or magazine but an object. Go ahead."

The little brat quickly replied, "A fully functional elevator!"

The crowd broke out in screaming laughter.

The poor clown stuttered for a moment then said, "How about you little girl? What would you like me to make?"

"A doggie!" she answered, giggling.

Rainbow wig quickly tied off a balloon dog figure then handed it to the little girl.

"Who is next?" she asked.

Though the clown show started off funny, it quickly dwindled into an ordinary animal balloon show.

Fiveish the man began fidgeting in his seat. He had had enough.

"Where are the jokes!" he yelled.

"Hey, that's not nice," said someone from behind.

Rainbow wig was losing her audience.

Fiveish the man saw some potential fun.

He chanted, "Do some shtick! Do some shtick! Do some shtick!"

Rainbow wig did not know what to do.

"Be quiet or get out of here!" said another from behind. "Show a little respect!"

Fiveish the man stood up and yelled with nasty sarcasm, "Ah, you're just another clown that walks around blowing up balloons!"

With that, the whole audience lost control. People tumbled over the seats; two ladies got into a wrestling match, children ran up onto the stage and rioted, some of them pulling out the speaker wires while others tried to tie the poor white faced clowns shoe laces together. The whole place was in an uproar.

But Fiveish the man with a huge grin on his face quietly sauntered away.

"Oh! Is that the exit?" he asked nobody in particular.

But before he reached it he stopped, turned around and looked back at Clown Alley.

"What an odd place this is," he thought. "It's not on any map of the city."

The carnival tents flapped in the gentle breeze while dozens of balloons floated across the strange sky. Carnival rides spun along their circular trajectories while a roller coaster rumbled along it wavy tracks.

"There's something odd about this place," he thought, "something slightly off."

Of course he would never consider that it was he, who was slightly off.

He couldn't quite describe the strangeness. The parents and children were not quite right. The breeze, balloons, and sky were inexplicably strange, but only a little bit. And what about that curious gypsy calling him to her tent?

"Where did it lead to?" he thought. "What is beyond that flap?" His heart raced. He almost decided to go running back to her and then through the opening in the tent.

He took a deep breath then sighed.

He turned to go but then noticed a hat sitting on its side alone on a park bench. He walked to the bench and looked down at the hat. It rocked back and forth in the breeze. It seemed as if it were alive and would stand up and walk away at any moment.

"Well what do you know, that's the Ringmasters top hat!" he said with astonishment.

He looked to see if anyone was watching then picked it up, studying it for a moment. He turned it around in his hands. The hat was made of stiff material, but the gray felt was soft to the touch much like peach fuzz. He looked inside the hat.

"Strange," he muttered. "I can't see the bottom of it."

He reached his hand inside the hat but suddenly felt his stomach turn. A feeling of nausea lightly overcame him. He put the hat back down then stepped away from it.

"Ah ha!" he said. "Now I know that the directions with the glow ink was the Ringmasters idea after all. He is surely up to something. I'll just leave his top hat right here. To see him desperately looking for it as the show is about to begin, would make me feel all warm and cozy inside."

But the smell of popcorn, bubble gum and cotton candy didn't smell so good anymore. In fact he felt like throwing up."

"That calliope music is eating my brain!"

He turned then went through the exit archway made of tangled ivy.

The lights, the sounds and the smells of the circus suddenly evaporated. Fiveish turned then looked back towards the exit. It wasn't there. He could only see a trash-ridden driveway fading into the shadows.

For a moment, he thought of investigating the

strange phenomenon of the disappearing archway, but then he realized how dark it was.

"I must hurry! The show is starting soon!"

He looked up and down the avenue.

"The Ringmasters directions are no good! He led me on a wild goose chase. What do I do now? Which way do I go?"

He was about to stop a passerby to ask for directions, but then he spotted it. There it was, the Mystique Theater directly across the street.

"Well, the directions were good after all," he murmured. "Humph, I still don't trust him."

Chapter Four
The Mystique Theater

H E RAN UP the ornate steps then stopped to scan the colossal building. Thick Roman pillars towered upward, bone white with veins of blue marbling holding a massive dome.

He quickly moved through the decorative double doors then through the luxurious lobby. The stage was magnificent; a beautiful red curtain stretched across the length of it.

Hundreds of plush seats filled the auditorium. There were three levels of fancy booths along the sidewalls with spiral staircases leading up to them. The steps were made of ivory and the bannisters made of ebony.

"This must have been an opera house in the old days."

The walls were lined with decorative gold plating. Mammoth sized paintings depicted great and historic events, though not historic events that he had ever learned about.

A battle was being waged in an emerald grotto deep underground. Green stalagmites and stalactites formed dangerous obstacles for the combatants. The soldiers were not human but frighteningly strange with countless oddities. A creature, a female, tall with long black hair, snow-white skin and black lidless eyes held an uplifted sword.

Another creature, tall and ready to pounce looked like a black panther.

"Is that a clown in the painting?" he gasped.

He stepped closer.

He had never seen nor heard nor even imagined that a clown could be a worrier, ready to give its life in battle. But this clown had its sword raised, and shield held out.

"I think that this artist needs to see a psychiatrist."

Hulking humanoid beasts with fangs were attacking the odd troupe of characters. The vision of the Clown Alley archway and its Japanese Kabuki masks flashed into his memory.

Then he spotted a human. He was sprawled on the grotto floor behind the clown. Now, he understood. The clown was protecting the human who was injured, bleeding and unconscious.

"This is mind-boggling!" he uttered.

He managed to pull himself away for the hour was late. But he made a point in his mind to revisit these magnificent paintings.

There were dozens of people milling about. There were camera operators, newspaper reporters and several stagehands setting up. Famous people including movie celebrities and movie producers were being led to special seats.

His heart began to flutter. This was his big chance, and he wasn't going to let anyone or anything get in his way.

He went backstage.

"Here's your dressing room, sir," said a young man.

"All right, now get lost," said Fiveish the Man.

"Here's your baggage, Fiveish," said a young girl.

"Put it over there and scram," said Fiveish the Man, again.

"Here are some children who would love to have your autograph."

"Tell them to beat it. I have no time for doing anybody any favors, and if you bother me again, I'll stick my clown shoe in your ear. Now leave!" said the man called Fiveish.

He stepped into his private dressing room and looked around. There was his tattered clown suitcase with all his props stuffed inside. His mirror with its ring of shining light bulbs was already set up on his makeup desk. Sitting on the desk was his dented old makeup kit that included all the colored grease paints that he would need, brushes and powder to seal his makeup so it would not smear. Also contained in the kit were his supply of makeup remover, cotton balls, Q-Tips, spirit gum and of course his red rubber clown nose. His freshly laundered costume was hanging on a hook on the door along with his black clown hat. His clown shoes were lying on the floor next to the makeup table.

First, he put his black clown pants on with its colorful patches. Then he slipped into his striped clown shirt. He pulled his suspenders over his shoulders to hold up his pants. He pulled on his striped socks. His red clown shoes were next.

He realized that he was already falling into character. He seemed to shrink in size. His shoulders became rounded with his neck forward a bit.

He sat at his makeup table. Looking into the mirror with the light bulbs, he studied his face for a moment.

First, using grease paint, he smeared on his white clown lips that gave him the sad friendly face that children loved. Then he put on the black makeup used for his scruffy hobo beard and for his sad eyebrows.

As he looked in the mirror, he saw a change take place from Fiveish the man to Fiveish the Clown. He started to relax. His shoulders drooped even more, and a friendly smile flashed across his face. Next, he put some blue under his eyes because Fiveish the Clown often looks like he is about to cry.

"And now for the finishing touch," he said to the mirror, "the nose."

He applied some spirit gum on the skin around the base of his nose then stuck it onto his face.

"Ah. I'm ready. A work of art."

Adjusting his clown hat just right and tightening its string under his chin, he left his changing room then hobbled towards the stage with his goofy clown walk. He had only a few minutes before the show started.

"Good luck Fiveish," said the sound director, "there's a big crowd out there waiting for you."

"Thank you very much," he said with a soft, friendly tone. "I appreciate it."

He was no longer thinking about money or boats or castles. All he wanted was to make the children and adults happy. He wanted to make everybody happy. He was a different person. He was no longer Fiveish the Man; he was now Fiveish the Clown.

Chapter Five
The Great Show

THE PALATIAL AUDITORIUM with its booths, balconies and mezzanine was filled to capacity. An immense chandelier half the size of the ceiling hung above the audience. There was an expectant hush as the theater lights dimmed and the curtain became illuminated with aqua blue, green and purple.

A squeaking noise could just be heard as the red curtain slowly opened. The stage had the colors of a carnival. The backdrop walls were painted with blue, green and orange diamonds. In the middle of the stage rested the circus center ring painted red.

The Ringmaster walked on stage then stepped into the center of the ring. Miraculously, he had his top hat back on his head as if it had never been misplaced. With his black handlebar mustache and the monocle covering his left eye, he looked at the audience with a devilish smile. He lifted his top hat and bowed.

"And now!" he belted out with a powerful voice, "Ladies and gentleman, boys and girls, what you have all been waiting for, that silly slouch, that gallant goof, the one, the only, your friend and mine, Fiveish the Clown!"

The auditorium was silent.

The velvety red curtain closed, hiding the Ringmaster from view then slowly opened again.

The clown walked on from the side of the stage pulling a huge commercial wet vac. His face was turned away from the audience as he pulled. When he stopped and slowly turned to face the audience, his eyes were closed.

The children giggled lightly.

When he opened his eyes and saw the filled theater, he shrieked then flew sideways like a spring.

The audience jumped in their seats.

He tried to run away but was captured by the Ringmaster and the Stagehand. They lifted him up and carried him back to center stage while his big clumsy clown feet dragged along the floor.

He was stood up then roughly dusted off. Looking at the audience, he took a deep breath then nervously smiled.

"Fiveish!" yelled the Ringmaster, "Vacuum the stage!"

The clown pointed at the Wet Vac.

"But there's no vacuum bag," he said.

You see, everybody in the world except for clowns, know that Wet Vacs do not have vacuum bags.

He scratched his head on top of his clown hat.

Suddenly, the clown smiled. He pulled from his

pocket a gigantic deflated balloon. This was not just a balloon; it was a BALLOON!

He slipped the balloon over the out-take valve on the side of the wet vac. He did this so it would work just like a vacuum bag, which would solve his problem, right? Right?

Smiling, he flipped the switch. The vacuum roared with the sound of a hurricane. The balloon bag quickly grew in size while the silly clown vacuumed the floor.

It grew bigger and bigger, but the little tramp was too busy vacuuming to notice. The audience began to laugh and gasp at the same time.

"Watch out!" they yelled. "Turn around Fiveish! Look behind you!"

But it was to no avail. He danced and flipped while vacuuming away.

It continued to grow until it was bigger than the grinning clown.

The uproarious laughter of the children grew louder than the storm-wind of the wet vac.

"Mommy, is he going to get hurt?" asked a child.

The balloon stretched to half the size of the stage.

"I don't think this is very safe," said a mother from the fourth row.

The children and adults in the first three rows of the theater were getting nervous; some were about to get up and run.

The balloon stretched and stretched.

"Run for your lives!" shouted someone from the front row.

Then it happened.

But before we get to what happened, you should know that Fiveish the Clown was a highly trained clown. The greatest clowns of his day trained him. He was trained in the ancient art of Comedia Dell'arte. He was a true professional; he was a true professional because he said it a lot and since he said it a lot, it was true, and since the word true has now been said three times in this sentence, it means that it is very true.

He was a master in the construction of a joke (jokes are called Lazzi in ancient clown talk.) He would sometimes add a joke to his routine that could have more than one punch line. His jokes could end up either one way or another way; both would be funny. This unknown quality added even more surprise to his shtick. And that is what is going to happen right now, so hold onto your seats.

Then it happened.

The balloon exploded. Fiveish flew into the air all the way to the side of the stage. The audience jumped from the noise. Confetti that was secretly put into the deflated balloon before the show flew every which way. Laughter filled the theater.

That was one possible outcome, but that is not what happened.

Then it happened.

The balloon stretched to the point of exploding, but instead it slipped off of the outtake piece of the wetvac. The balloon flew into the air with a very loud and funny bathroom noise. It hit the ceiling then wobbled every which way over the audience, spilling its confetti onto their upturned faces.

Laughter and cheer arose.

That was the possible second outcome, but that is not what happened either, which was a surprise to the clown because there was only supposed to be two possible outcomes.

This is what actually happened:

Then it happened.

The giant balloon slipped off, flew into the air towards the ceiling, moved across it while blowing out its confetti onto the audience. But then, it got pulled into the air conditioning duct and through the pipes. It shot out through the air conditioner with an explosion of confetti that made the theater look like it was caught in a snow blizzard. The confetti was so thick that the audience could not even see the ceiling. Finally, the confetti drifted down on top of the spectators.

Wonder and laughter was in the air.

But where was the clown?

"Help!" came a muffled voice.

There he was. The balloon explosion from the air conditioner caused the backdrops to fall down on top of the poor little clown, pinning him to the wooden stage floor.

"Help!"

The audience burst forth with laughter.

He tried to get out from under the wreckage, but he couldn't; he was stuck like glue.

With every struggle, the audience laughed and laughed.

"Can somebody help me please?"

The wonderful though strange thing is, if this joke or lazzi had been planned, it would never have worked, mainly because it was too dangerous. It was one of those strange flukes that rarely happen during a performance that can either ruin the show or make it truly great. This time it was truly magnificent.

"It's all part of the show folks," said the Ringmaster with a fake smile as he and the Stagehand lifted the heavy backdrops off the clown.

He was bruised and battered but the children and adults loved it. They rose to their feet for a standing ovation.

Fiveish the clown was now a true comedy star. He was a true star because he was now a very true star and not because it was said three times. This performance made him a TRUE STAR.

The clown painfully bowed, rubbed his back then with the help of the Ringmaster and Stagehand limped off the stage.

The curtain closed bringing an end to act one. The theater lights brightened then the audience got up for an intermission.

The crowd made their way towards the lobby to buy some soda and popcorn. Children giggled as they shook the confetti from their hair and off their shoulders.

The cleanup crew quickly entered the theater to sweep the confetti off the seats and floor. They lifted the backdrops, securing them into their proper position.

Fiveish the clown was brought back to his changing room. He was laid down onto some cushions. An ice pack was quickly brought and placed on his ribs. He was in terrible pain.

It is a pitiful thing to see a clown with his costume and makeup on grimacing in pain from an injury.

The Ringmaster stood in the corner of the room almost hidden in shadow. He had a strange look on his face. His right eyebrow was lifted, but the eye behind the monocle seemed to gleam with light. He began tapping the side of his top hat.

"Click, click, click," went the top hat as if a signal in Morse code was being sent out.

AFTER THE INTERMISSION, the audience eagerly took their seats.

The Ringmaster walked on stage. He looked at the audience and said with a mighty voice, "Is it Oneish?

The children answered, "No!"

"Is it Twoish?"

"No!"

"Is it Threeish?"

"No!"

"Is it Fourish?"

"No!

"Well, then what time is it?"

"It's Fiveish, hooray!"

"Yep, it sure is, yuk-yuk-yuk."

The lights dimmed.

"Ladies and gentleman, boys and girls, if you look towards the center ring you will see an extraordinary clown extravaganza like you've never seen before. Watch in amazement as David battles Goliath!"

The stage went dark. Then a spotlight appeared in the center with the little clown standing in the middle of it. He looked at the audience then waved with a smile.

Some explanation is needed here: The little tramp clown was in pain. The backdrops were heavy, and Fiveish was hurt from the crash. But he deeply understood and believed in the ancient phrase, "The show must go on!" It was difficult, but he acted as if he were uninjured and smiled and played as if nothing happened, because that is what true professional artists do.

The spotlight grew in size revealing a massive bed.

He yawned a fantastically big yawn, so big in fact, that his mouth looked like a wide cave. He then jumped up onto the bed. He pulled the covers up then began to snore. The snore got louder and louder until it vibrated off the walls of the theater.

The children giggled.

Dreamy harp music could be heard piping in as Fiveish fell into a deep sleep. Fog rolled onto the stage. The lights dimmed to a mysterious aquarium blue.

Suddenly, there was a flash of lightning and an

explosion of thunder. The frightened clown sat up with a start, his heart beating like a scared mouse. The audience also jumped from the suddenness of it.

"What happened?" blurted the clown.

Drum beats could be heard in the distance, then the sound of marching.

"Hey! Who are those people marching this way?"

Ancient soldiers, armor clad with sword and shield, marched onto the stage followed by musicians with drum and cymbal, flute and horn. The last to enter the stage was a stilt-walking giant.

"I am Goliath," he growled with a thundering voice.

He had a shabby black beard that almost reached the floor.

Fiveish looked at the audience then gulped.

The drumming grew louder as the giant marched closer.

Goliath plunged his spear forward, but the clown ducked, ran between his legs and kicked him in the rear end.

"Oh Yea, well I am King David," said the clown. So take that!"

The giant thrust his spear again, but he flipped over it. The giant roared and thrust once more, but he ducked then crawled inside the cuff of the giant's baggy pant leg.

"Get out of there you tumbling buffoon!" huffed the stilt-walking colossus.

He tickled the giant's leg.

Screaming with laughter he begged the clown to stop.

Suddenly, the drumming stopped, the laughter died and then there was silence.

Faintly at first, then louder, the sound of ripping could be heard. A gaping hole was being torn in the giant's pant leg.

The little clown popped his clown face out through the hole, looked at the audience, smiled and said, "Knock, knock."

The audience replied, "Who's there?"

The clown answered, "P."

The audience, laughing so much they could barely speak, asked, "P who?"

The clown pinched his nose with his fingertips then answered, "Pee-yew, it smells in here."

The clown crawled out of the hole, ran to the side, turned then jumped off a mini trampoline into the air. He flew in a swan dive over Goliath, landing onto a soft crash pad.

Please excuse me for this important but brief announcement: These days, we do not use the term, "crash pad." It seems that the word, "crash," is too frightening for little children. So be careful for now on and only use the alternate term, "safety cushion." We don't want our children to cry from fright now do we?

He quickly shot the giant with a slingshot hitting him in the forehead. Goliath fell to the floor, which isn't easy to do when you're on stilts.

The audience cheered.

The fog rolled in again, hiding the stage. The music and lights faded. The drums sounded farther and farther away, while the sound of marching dwindled into the distance.

The lights returned. The fog had blown away. The clown was on his bed yawning and smiling.

"That sure was an exciting dream," he said.

Tossing the blanket away, he bounced up and down on the bed. With a double back flip, he landed safely onto the floor.

The curtain closed at the end of the show. But then the clown parted the curtain just a little. Slipping through, he faced the audience for his curtain call. It was dark, only the spotlight surrounded him in a tight circle. He smiled, took a deep bow then said to the audience, "Thank you. Good night."

He slipped back again behind the curtain.

The audience shouted, "We want Fiveish! We want Fiveish!"

The lights came back on, a signal for everyone to get up and exit the auditorium but the audience didn't leave.

The producers, directors and theatrical critics in the audience were absolutely captivated by the performance. The smiles on their faces made them look like children. In fact, they felt like children.

Finally, the lights dimmed again, and Fiveish came back out for an encore bow. The audience became silent. He was limping and holding his side.

Suddenly, the clown kicked up into a handstand,

looked at the audience upside-down then jumped in a circle on one hand.

The audience cheered.

With his feet back down on Earth, he looked out at the sea of smiling faces. A tear formed at the corner of his eye; he blinked and it rolled down his cheek. The audience saw this and slowly began to get up on their feet for a standing ovation.

When they finally became quiet, Fiveish said with a cracked voice, "Thank you again. You've been so kind. Good night to you my dear friends."

He slipped behind the curtain for the last time.

The audience stood in silence.

At first only a few people clapped but in a few seconds the entire theater was in an uproar.

After the last person left the theater, there was complete silence.

THE CURTAIN WAS closed, but Fiveish was still on stage standing behind it. He was alone. Oddly, the Ringmasters top hat sat in the middle of the center ring. A strange glow emanated from within its depths.

There he stood with his face unmoving, staring at the back of the red curtain. Its folds swayed back and forth touched by an invisible breeze secretly finding its way under doors, rusty vents or small cracks in the ancient walls of the old opera house.

Something was wrong.

He felt dizzy. His vision became blurred. He was

beginning to see strange images moving and flickering on the back of the curtain as if it were a movie screen.

Then he saw the image of Fiveish the man floating on the back of the curtain, a scary image. A swoon began to envelop him. He didn't want to become the man. He was afraid of the man.

"No!" he pleaded.

The room began to spin then tilt. He stumbled and fell to the floor. And then all was dark.

Chapter Six
Metamorphosis

H E AWOKE ON the dressing room couch. How he got there, he knew not. He turned the light on then walked into the hallway. Looking to the left then to the right, the theater seemed empty. He quickly moved back into the dressing room and locked the door.

Still in his costume, he searched for his street clothes, but he couldn't find them.

"What is going on?"

He walked over to the mirror; his makeup was still on. He pulled at his nose to remove it, but it wouldn't come off

"Strange, I didn't think I put on that much spirit gum."

He reached for some makeup remover, put a little on a cloth then rubbed his face to remove the grease-paint. When he was finished, he looked in the mirror again. No change, the makeup was still on his face just as before.

"This is really weird."

This time he used warm water and soap then again looked into the mirror.

"I don't understand. Why isn't it coming off?"

He grabbed his clown nose with a tight grip then repeatedly tried to yank it off his face, but the pain was too much for him.

Fear welled up inside of him; he was trembling.

"What is happening to me?"

The clown face would not come off; it was stuck to his face. It wasn't just stuck, it was his face, and it was real. The clown face was a real face.

Unlocking the dressing room door, he ran out into the hallway.

"Help!" he shouted. "Somebody help me! Please!"

But there was only silence.

He made his way to the stage. Shadows from the backdrops loomed menacingly. The curtain slowly moved as if it were alive.

He dropped onto his knees.

"This can't be real," he whispered.

He crawled under the curtain to look out at the empty theater.

He heard a noise out in the auditorium.

"Who's there?"

Someone started laughing.

"Who are you? Let me see you!" he shouted.

More people began laughing.

"Stop laughing at me!" he cried.

Soon the entire theater was filled with laughter. But the theater was empty.

"Why are you laughing? Stop it I say!"

He jumped off the stage then ran out to the seats, falling and tripping as he went.

"Where are you? Come out and let me see you!"

He ran up the steps to the mezzanine. He looked under the rows of seats. Then he ran up a winding staircase to check one of the booths.

Exhausted, he sat on a cushioned seat then laid his head against the back of it.

"Leave me alone," he quietly moaned. Then softer as if it were an echo he repeated, "Leave me alone."

His eyelids became heavy.

"It has to be a nightmare," he thought as he dozed into a fitful sleep.

Chapter Seven
The Nightmare Begins

H E WOKE UP late the next morning.
"I'm sure it was just an awful dream."
He gave a tug to his nose.

"No, it can't be real."

He ran down the spiral staircase then jumped up onto the stage. Slipping through the curtain, he then ran along the hall towards his changing room.

His legs were bowed; his shoulders were rounded and his feet pointed outward.

"I've turned into a real clown," he said in disbelief.

Running into his changing room, he quickly looked into the mirror.

Again he tried to remove the makeup but to no avail. Reaching down, he grabbed a clown shoe and pulled.

"It's stuck!"

He paced back and forth.

"Okay, calm down, breath. Think this through. This has to be a dream, there's no other explanation. So I'll just recline here on the couch until I wake up."

Hours went by. Hunger began to claw at his insides. By lunchtime, he couldn't take it any longer; he needed to have some food.

He left his room then ran to the front entrance of the theater. Daylight shined in through the crack between the double doors. He pushed but they wouldn't budge.

He ran to the back of the theater, found the rear exit then pushed. The door swung open.

He stepped through the doorway and into a back alley filled with junk. He hid behind a large trashcan near the entrance of the crowded street.

He took a deep breath then said, "Well, here it goes. Ladies and gentlemen, boys and girls, here comes Fiveish, the Clown!"

He moped out onto the crowded sidewalk.

"Look Tommy, a little clown!"

He made his way to the street corner.

As soon as he was noticed an audience formed in a circle.

More heads turned, and people began to run to watch the street show. Soon, there was a crowd surrounding him, already beginning to laugh.

He waited for silence, then said, "Eh... Hi." The audience started laughing.

"Listen!" he said. "I'm not trying to be funny right now, really I'm not."

More laughter.

"You have to believe me; I'm serious."

There were wails of laughter.

"Please!"

Every word he said was driving the audience into hysterics.

"It's not that funny!" he yelled.

There was something odd about their laughter. It was abnormal; it was over the top. They seemed a little nutso.

"Blip," he said.

Laughter.

"Schnitzel."

Laughter.

"Gefilte Fish."

More laughter.

"I've got to get out of here," he whispered.

He tried to run through the throng of people, but they just pushed him back into the circle. They wanted to see him do his shtick.

"What am I going to do?" He whimpered.

He ran then dove low to get through their legs. Suddenly, a lady grabbed him by his suspenders and pulled him back.

"You're not going to get away that easy smiley," she said, as she roughly hurled him back to the center of the circle.

Their laughter was frightening. Their faces were turning red.

He tried another desperate attempt to get away but a big teenager blocked him.

"Where do you think you're going laughy," he said with his hands on his hips and a snarl on his lips.

A little hand reached up and squeezed his nose. It honked loudly.

"Ouch, that hurt!" cried the clown. But the crowd just laughed and laughed.

Another hand reached up and squeezed it. Out came a painful squeak.

"Keep your little hands off me you mean children!" he yelled, but the red faced laughter just got louder and louder.

"Pull his rubber nose off," screamed a child and soon a dozen kids were reaching for it.

The whole crowd was chanting, "Pull the clown's nose off! Pull the clown's nose off! Pull the clown's nose off!"

"It's a madhouse!" he cried. "I'm in an asylum!"

Just then, a police officer came by to see what the disturbance was.

The clown quickly yelled out, "Mister Police Officer, can you help me please?"

Officer Dooley pushed his way through the crowd.

"What is it little fella?" he said with a smile.

"I'm in big trouble. I can't get away from these people. Can you help me?"

"Listen to me Mr. Clown," he said. "You've got some trick up your sleeve, and I'm not falling for it."

The clown was desperate. Suddenly, an idea popped into his head.

"Okay," the clown said. "In that case, you have left me no choice."

He lifted his clown shoe into the air then stomped onto officer Dooley's toes.

He didn't want to do it; he never wanted to hurt anybody, but he could think of nothing else that would get him out of there. And besides, this was only a dream, right?

"Ouch!" howled the police officer as he jumped in a circle on one foot. The audience laughed and laughed.

Officer Dooley chased the scared clown around the circle of screaming children and adults. He grabbed the clown by the back of his shirt and pulled him through the crowd.

Their hands were pink from clapping while they watched the clown get ruffed up.

The officer cuffed him then aggressively led him into the back of his police car. The sad clown looked out the back window as they pulled away.

As a mother watched the sad faced clown staring back at them from the police car window, her little daughter said, "Mommy, mommy! Funny, funny!" while her teenage son said, "What a dumb clown!"

At every stoplight, adults and children turned their heads in amazement to see the unusual sight of a clown in a squad car being taken to jail.

"Now, why did you have to go and stomp on my foot like that?" asked Officer Dooley. "What did I ever do to you? You could have just asked me, and I might have been a volunteer for you."

Officer Dooley pulled over in front of the police precinct. He opened the car door then led the clown up the steps.

"Look!" cried someone from the sidewalk. "There's a clown in handcuffs being taken to jail!"

Soon, there was a crowd of people with their cell phones out videoing the unusual sight. Two ladies pushed their way next to the clown then took selfies. In moments, microphones and television cameras were stuffed into his face. Officer Dooley was desperately trying to get to the front door of the precinct, but the crowd became too thick.

"What were you arrested for?" asked a newsperson.

"Why are you in handcuffs?" asked another. "Are you an evil clown?"

But the clown was too depressed and frightened to answer.

Soon, photos and video of Fiveish the Clown in handcuffs being escorted into police headquarters became viral.

The live stream of the event was watched by the Peoples Republic of China, Bangladesh, Zimbabwe, Kamchatka, and Timbuktu. People all over the world were asking, "Who is that clown?"

Someone in the crowd threw a gooey cheese danish that hit poor officer Dooley square between his eyes.

"I'm having a bad day," said the officer.

Fiveish was too upset to say to Officer Dooley that his day was about one thousand times worse.

When they finally squeezed through the door and

entered the police station, the other officers began to laugh when they saw the clown.

"Awe, poor clown," they said. "What did he do?"

"He stepped on my foot," said Officer Dooley pouting.

The police in the station burst into laughter. Then they laughed even more when they saw pieces of sticky cheese danish stuck to his face.

"Let him go," they said, giggling. "Can't you see he wouldn't hurt a fly? Let the clown go."

The frustrated and embarrassed police officer brought him outside through the rear door, let go of his shirt then gave him a kick.

"And don't let me see your sad clown face again."

Chapter Eight
On the Run

THE LITTLE CLOWN took a quiet street. Trying to stay hidden, he ducked behind cars, trashcans and fences. He made his way towards the nearest grocery store. He was very hungry.

Children and teenagers all over the neighborhood had just finished watching on their cell phones and tablets the events unfold at the local police precinct. It had caused quite a stir.

One little boy was just taking his first bite of a cream cheese and black liquorice bagel when he spotted the sneaking clown through his kitchen window. He dropped the bagel to the floor, smiled, showing his black teeth then quickly ran and opened the front door squashing the bagel as he went. He ran out onto the porch leaving black liquorice footprints on his parent's new carpet and yelled out at the top of his lungs, "CLOWN!!!"

Apartment doors flew open as neighborhood children sprinted towards Fiveish.

"Get him!" they howled. "Get the clown!"

"Help!" screamed the terrified clown.

He ran as fast as his floppy clown feet could carry him.

Down the street, he sprinted with a wild mob of drooling kids in hot pursuit.

He dodged around a parked car then sped down a driveway between two brownstone apartments.

The horde of raving youngsters chased him into the driveway causing a bottleneck that slowed them all down.

This was his chance. He ran then jumped onto a station wagon then dived through the air grabbing the bottom rung of a fire escape ladder.

Being a trained acrobat, with another couple of jumps he was standing on the roof of the three-story apartment building.

He looked down at the mob of crazed kids who were trying to find a way to get at him, to get at his red nose.

"What is the matter with you?" he yelled down.

Running along the top of the brownstones, he was a strange colorful figure jumping from one building to the next.

Today's teenagers and young adults would call the clowns antics Parkour or Free Running, which was originally practiced in France. But most people did not know that Fiveish the Clown was one of the greatest Parkour practitioners. In the old days it was called Urban Gymnastics.

He remembered his first flip off the side of a tree when he was only 6 years old.

The clown climbed, swung and flipped his way high above the screaming children. He jumped and caught the branch of a tree.

Jumping from tree to tree, he made it to another apartment complex. The clown could have been mistaken for a chimpanzee.

There was a swimming pool down below. Several people were lounging about; some were swimming. He spotted a diving board. It was far, but he was confident that he could make it. He backed up then ran with all his might. He jumped and flew through the air. But just before he landed on the diving board, a lady stepped onto it. His clown shoes hit the board right next to the ladies bare feet and at the exact same time.

Now, let's take a moment to understand what is happening here: When two insane people purposely bounce on a trampoline at the same time and in just about the same place, their combined weight will cause them to fly twice as high. This gives them the airtime to do multiple flips and twists. In trampoline terminology, it is called a "double bounce." It is a very dangerous technique, one that has caused not a few back and knee injuries and the end of the careers of some of the greatest gymnasts, acrobats, and parkour aficionados.

The clown was very aware of this, but it was a split-second decision, and he was no ordinary acrobat.

The clown landed onto the diving board with the full extra weight of the lady. The board bent more than it had ever bent before. Then with tremendous force, it snapped up more than it had ever snapped up before.

The two of them flew through the air like limp

rag dolls over the pool and across the cemented area. They landed on the shade awning. The whole contraption collapsed. Several retirees relaxing on their lounge chairs in the shade were suddenly plunged into complete darkness from the heavy awning fabric that fell on them.

"It's another blackout Henry."

"It's the middle of the day Ruthy; it's not a blackout. It's a solar eclipse."

Suddenly, the fabric lifted up and off the people leaving them sprawling on the floor or upside down on their lounge chairs. The awning fabric mysteriously moved across the grass and over the fence like a ghost in the wind.

When the clown was out of sight, he tossed the awning off then dodged down the street. He had lost the crazed kids that were chasing him. He could hear their banshee howls getting farther and farther away.

Hiding behind bushes, hedges, and trees, he slowly crept his way towards the grocery store.

He was tired and hungry. All he could think of was food.

He walked into the grocery store and began searching the isles. Heads turned to look at the goofy figure as he meandered along looking at chips, candy, popcorn and soda. He settled for a peach, a nectarine, a banana and a quart of milk.

A little girl holding her mother's dress said, "looky mommy a silly clown. Can I squeeze your nose?"

The clown froze for a moment, grimacing from the

recent memory then slowly scooted away not trusting the kid.

He stood in line waiting for his turn at the cash register. People looked at him strangely, most were snickering, but some eyed him with suspicion.

You see most people only like clowns while they are performing, while they do tricks, stunts and jokes. People enjoy clowns when they juggle, make animal balloons, do magic tricks or act silly. But generally, people do not like clowns very much or are uncomfortable with them when they are filling their car tank with gas, spackling a wall, entering an airplane, programming an app or buying groceries. Normal things that people do in life are abnormal for clowns and not funny. One thing for sure is that a clown should never ever be serious. And as some clowns know all too well, if you are not funny you had better stop your show and get off stage as fast as you can before the children get angry at you.

Here are some examples of clown hate mail from children that were not amused:

"You're not funny!"

"I hate clowns!"

"Pull that wig off your stupid clown head."

"You freak me out."

"What a stupid clown!"

"I would like to rip that silly clown nose off your face!"

The lady at the register nervously laughed, then

said, "I thought Halloween was October thirty-first, ha ha. It's two dollars and twenty-six cents."

Fiveish felt for his wallet, but it wasn't there.

"I forgot that I am wearing my clown pants," said the clown with disappointment, "I'll be right back."

Leaving the groceries, he quickly ran out the door.

It was getting late in the afternoon, and he still hadn't eaten yet. Most banks close at three. If he raced as fast as he could, he might just make it to the bank before they lock the doors.

Many heads turned to look as a strange little clown raced through the city streets with his red nose leaning into the wind and giant feet flapping along the pavement.

Slipping through the bank door just as they were about to lock it, he went to the end of the line.

"Look, Mommy!" said a little boy, "a clown, a funny clown."

Again, the clown froze with fear but tried not to show it.

"Do a trick, do a trick for me, okay, Mr. Clown?"

Fiveish the clown was not in a good clown mood. But he slowly bent down and said; "You can squeeze my nose but please don't hurt me okay. Please be gentle."

The little boy gently squeezed and it made the sound of a loud squeaky honk. He quickly drew his hand away then laughed out loud. Fiveish was relieved. The other people in line thought it was charming and giggled along with the little boy.

The clown was beginning to relax.

"Maybe things will turn out okay after all," he thought.

Then it was his turn.

"I would like to take out twenty dollars please."

The bank teller looked at him suspiciously.

"Your name please."

"My name is Fiveish."

Looking at him more closely with a frown beginning to grow on her face, she said, "I need your last name."

"Oh, It's Fiveish... eh... oh dear, I don't know; I can't remember what my last name is. I'm known as Fiveish the Clown."

"Your account number," she requested, as the frown on her face turned into a look of fear.

You see, at a bank when someone wearing a mask walks in and starts asking for money with no name, bank tellers may think that they are about to be robbed. So, after she found out that he also didn't have an account number, she slowly reached under the counter and pushed a little red button.

At that moment, the sound of a loud alarm began to ring. The clown looked around at the people still in the bank and saw that they were all looking at him and that they were frightened.

He tried to smile, then said, "Come on, you don't think that I'm going to rob you, do you?"

But that is exactly what they thought.

"I'm just a friendly clown," he whimpered. "I'm not a burglar!"

When the people in the bank heard him say the word "burglar," they started to scream and run and crash into each other.

The little boy said, "But Mommy, he's my friend."

"Stay away from him," she shrieked. "He's a bad clown!"

"I am not a bad clown!" he yelled with a broken cry as if from a tortured soul.

Police burst through the doors with their guns out, pointing at the little clown. An officer tried to grab him but he ducked under his arms then crawled between his legs. Another tried to dive on him, but the clown jumped into the air and grabbed a light fixture that hung from the ceiling by a chain. Back and forth he swung like a trapeze swinger at the circus. The police tripped over each other trying to grab his clown shoes high above their heads.

"Get him!"

They placed a chair under the clowns swinging feet. A policeman stepped up onto the chair in order to reach the clown, but the clown kicked the officer who then plummeted to the ground.

"Sorry."

Another officer grabbed his clown shoes. This time both of them swung back and forth until the light fixture ripped from the ceiling. The policeman flew head first into a wastepaper basket.

The clown flipped from the light then landed sitting on a patrolman's shoulders.

"Get off me!" he yelled. "And stop clowning around!"

The clown jumped onto the shoulders of another officer then jumped from officer to officer causing a big hullabaloo.

"You're a real pest; you know that?" said the officer who's cap dangled from his ear.

Then the clown dove through the window where the frightened bank clerk sat. The glass may have been bullet proof, but it didn't stop the clown from getting through. There are very few things in this world that are clown-proof.

A dozen police officers charged towards the little clown who just managed to slip into the giant steel bank vault.

Swinging the heavy vault door shut, then spinning the wheel to lock it, the clown sat on the cold metal floor. Shelves stuffed with tall stacks of money surrounded him. He was shivering. Banging and yelling could faintly be heard coming from the other side. He looked around. There was no way out.

Alarming thoughts raced through his clown brain: "How did I get into this horrible mess?"

A tear formed in his clown eye.

"Am I going to go to prison? How are clowns treated in prison? Do they have a clown jail cell? Do they have a special prison block for clowns, separating them from the rest of the prison population? Is there a clown gang in prison that I can join for protection? Will the other inmate in my cell be a clown? And if not, will he have a good sense of humor? Do convicts smile at clowns or do they hate them? Will he laugh or beat me up when I do something funny?

He looked up towards the ceiling, "Woe is me," he whimpered.

Then a hopeful thought came to mind: "Wait a minute; this is only a nightmare. It's a very real nightmare, but it is still only a nightmare."

He stood up.

"Ha ha!" he laughed, swinging open the thick vault door. Smiling, he bowed as if the police were his audience.

He was tackled.

They grabbed him, handcuffed him, roughly threw him into a squad car and brought him to the police station again.

The little clown was already bumped and bruised; now he was really bumped and bruised.

"This doesn't feel like a nightmare anymore."

The police chief looked at him then said, "What? You again? This is supposed to be the dangerous masked bank robber that everybody is scared of? Ha-ha! Listen to me clowny. I'm going to let you go just one more time. But if I see your sorry clown face again, it's off to jail for you! Do you understand? Now go!"

Chapter Nine
Isador Elsenplace

I T WAS NIGHTTIME, it was cold and the clown was alone. He had no place to go, no one to talk to, and he was hungry with no money. A light snow began to fall.

He wandered slowly through the dark street, a bent shadowy figure. He did not have a happy clown face.

If one were to gaze upon the footprint's left in the snow, one might wonder, is it a Gorilla? Is it the Sasquatch? Could it be the Abominable Snowman? Or perhaps it's the Yeti or the Big Foot Monster?

No, it was only a big foot clown.

He made his way back to the Mystique Theater, he tried the front door, but he already knew that it was locked. He wandered over to the back entrance in the alley behind. Pulling on the back door he found that it wouldn't budge either. He was locked out.

The snow began to fall with more strength. With no coat on he began to shiver.

He sat on the cement steps. Sadness overwhelmed him as he pondered his misfortune.

Something fell in the darkness of the alleyway. It

made a slow rattling sound as it moved towards him. When it appeared from the gloom he saw that it was only an empty string bean can, but he was terrified.

There were footsteps approaching. Fiveish hid himself in the shadow at the side of the steps. Then he heard incoherent mumbling.

"Fire, fire, fire, up, up, up, I can't, I can't"

A man wearing a stained hat, ragged pants and a torn shirt came forward. If he had make-up on his face, he would have looked like a very tall tramp clown.

Fiveish stepped out of the shadow.

"Are you okay?" he asked.

"Help, scary," said the man when he saw the clown face. "Don't hurt me."

"I'm not going to hurt you, I promise," said Fiveish.

"Not Halloween," said the tattered man.

He squeezed his head between his hands as if he had a terrible headache.

"Not Halloween, not Halloween," he repeated.

"For me," said the clown, "every moment that I am stuck in this nightmare it's Halloween."

He reached out to shake hands.

The old man grabbed it then slowly brought it to his eyes.

"Clown hand," he said.

Examining it closely, he turned it around and checked each finger.

"Not scary," he said, and then shook it.

"I'm Fiveish the Clown.

"Izzy," said the old man letting go of the clown's hand then continuing past him deeper into the alley and deeper into the gloom.

The clown followed.

"Spooky," said Izzy pointing to the back door of the Mystique as he passed it by.

A smelly dumpster stood to the left and a decomposed car with its guts hanging out, ripped seat fabric and stripped wires on the right. They approached a dead catamaran, one float broken in half, the other a gaping hole.

A cinder block wall covered in ivy stretched along the alley. A small cardboard box rested on the pavement near it. Izzy opened the lid, stepped inside then vanished.

The clown stood for a moment pondering what just happened.

We all know the trick where dozens of circus performers climb inside a tiny clown car that shouldn't fit even one. But it would be a fine trick for a full-grown man to step into a small cardboard box and disappear into it.

The clown hesitantly put his foot into the box.

If you have ever heard the phrase "curiosity killed the cat," and you believed that it actually did, then you would not have stepped into that cardboard box. Nor would you walk into an old copper mine that was rickety and unstable. Nor would you peer over a thousand-foot cliff while standing on a loose boulder. Nor would you stand in front of a speeding locomotive to see if you could jump out of the way in time.

Clowns do not know of the phrase "Curiosity killed the cat." That is why clowns always get into trouble.

The clown stepped down a dilapidated ladder then followed a dripping tunnel under the cinderblock wall to the other side. Another ladder went up through a trap door into a room made from cardboard refrigerator boxes.

A match began to glow. Izzy touched it to an oil lamp sitting on a small table. The room was lit up with warm light.

A Persian carpet lined the floor. Three walls displayed beautiful works of art. The fourth wall was covered with old books of every size and color.

"Home," said Izzy, lighting another match then igniting some tinder in a dented metal garbage can. He blew on the small flame. The smoke went up a rusty stovepipe and out of the cardboard house. Soon a warm fire was aglow.

Filling two tin cups with water, the old man hung them over the flame. The heat from the glowing garbage can took the chill out of the air.

Izzy led the way through a rip in the cardboard.

The next room was made out of car windshields, collected from a junkyard.

There were flowering plants, fruit trees and vegetables of every kind growing inside like a jungle. In the middle of the glass room stood an ancient telescope.

Izzy pointed his finger up.

Glass windows from a condemned mansion long ago flattened to the ground formed the domed ceiling.

The clown looked through the eyepiece of the telescope and out through the glass ceiling. The sky had cleared and thousands of stars were gleaming in the night sky. Jupiter and rusty Mars were showing off their brilliance. Then a shooting star flew past, then another. Suddenly, hundreds of shooting stars zipped by.

"Izzy! What's happening?" cried the clown.

Izzy looked up. He became agitated.

"Fire, fire, fire, up, up, up, I can't," cried Izzy.

He put his hands on his temples then walked in a circle.

"Can't remember, can't think."

He followed Izzy back to the living room. Stationed in the corner stood a chair with its stuffing coming out.

The lamp gave a bright, cheery glow to Izzy's cardboard house. It lit up the paintings that covered almost every inch of the walls.

He looked from canvas to canvas. Scrawled on the bottom right corner of each was the signature, PARLUSION. They were beautiful and unique, depicting planets, far away galaxies, ancient castles and mysterious lands. But why were they here? Why were they hanging from cardboard boxes? They should have been in homes or art museums. Why didn't the world know about Parlusion?

Sitting on the soft chair and given a steaming cup

of tea, the little clown's soul was warmed. He picked up a book from the lamp stand.

The title read:

WORMHOLE TO OUTER SPACE
EASY CONSTRUCTION USING SIMPLE HOUSEHOLD MATERIALS

By
ISADOR ELSENPLACE

"You wrote this?" asked the clown.

But Izzy did not answer. He turned his face away.

The clown looked at the bookcases lining the cardboard walls. There was an entire shelf of books written by Izzy. There was:

HOW TO GET TO THE PLANET JUPITER
IN TEN MINUTES OR LESS

PLANT A TREE ON NEPTUNE
WITH THE EASY 1-2 DIMENSION WARP MACHINE

There were books written by Izzy on history, physics, chemistry and acting.

"Acting?" asked the clown.

"Can't remember, can't remember," frustration showed on his face.

"You used to be an actor?"

"I can't! Stop! Nothing, nothing," said Izzy; he seemed angry. "No memory," he said, and then broke into tears."

"Why, you're like me," said the clown, "living in a nightmare with no past, only small flashing memories, hints that lead to nowhere."

The clown pulled out another large volume; it was titled:

PHYSICS AND THE UNIVERSE
WITHOUT MATH

On the inside flap was a photo of Izzy sporting a black mustache. Standing behind him in the photo were two people. The clown looked closer. Were they actually people? They were not! But what were they? They did not look human nor did they look like any creature from Earth.

The clown rose from the couch chair then stepped close to one of the paintings. There was something oddly familiar about it.

The painting depicted a battlefield. A massive spaceship hovered over a white dome. So large was the ship that it seemed to fill the horizon. The dome was cracked; funnels of black smoke escaped into the sky. Through the jagged fracture could be seen toppled buildings, many of them broken into rubble. On top of the dome stood a lone figure with long black hair pointing his sword into the sky challenging the spaceship.

"Izzy!" the clown called out with excitement. "Now I know where I saw that style painting before. It's the same artist whose works are displayed on the walls of the Mystique Theater Opera House!"

Izzy turned in circles, his hands in his pockets.

"Scary place, scary place," he whimpered. "I can't, I can't," he repeated over and over again.

Who is Parlusion? He must be famous but I've never heard of him.

The clown put the old book back down onto the table.

A piece of paper slipped out. It floated down onto the Persian rug. Lifting it he read:

To my dear son, Isador:

Do not forget who you once were or the great achievements you accomplished at such a young age and for such a short time. For I, your loving mother had you under my watchful eye till you were snatched away from me, never to be seen again.

To unravel the secret of who you really are and to remember all the wonderful and mighty deeds that you have done, seek out the great King Almar and his Troubadours.

With both sadness and deep affection for my beautiful and pure son: your loving mother:

Elsie Elsenplace

The clown handed the note to Izzy, he refused to take it; he was very wound up. He began to shake and mumble to himself. His face started to turn red.

"It's okay Izzy; everything is going to be all right. There is a reason for all of this, for you and for me."

The clown's stomach rumbled with hunger.

"Come on, let's get some food. The vegetables in your greenhouse won't be enough for us. Follow me."

A TALL MAN in ragged clothing lurched across the street with a little clown by his side.

"After I bow at the end of the show," whispered the clown, "take your hat off and bring it near the spectators. They'll fill it with money."

The marquee above the ticket booth displayed the title of the evening's world premier film:

IMP

THEY PUSHED THEIR way through the throng of patrons who eagerly awaited the doors to swing open.

"Oops," said Izzy.

"Sorry," said the clown.

They turned to face their captive audience, lining the sidewalk in front of the theater entrance.

Fiveish's heart suddenly jumped in his chest.

"They're not human!" he moaned.

A cavalcade of creepy clowns stretched along the

sidewalk. One had a hatchet buried in its skull another wielded a chainsaw.

"Scary clowns," said Izzy.

A particularly sinister looking clown with a butcher knife stuck in its neck turned his attention towards Izzy.

"Hey that dude looks like Frankenstein," he said.

"Not monster," said Izzy.

The audience laughed.

Izzy looked over at Fiveish.

"Not monster!" he repeated in despair.

The clown jumped up then stood on Izzy's shoulders.

As usual Izzy's face remained frozen.

Fiveish lifted the hat off Izzy's head then began juggling it with three eggs.

With your permission, I have a significant clown note: clowns have very large pockets filled with all sorts of outlandish props. If one were to pick a clowns pocket, one would be surprised to find an endless array of oddities: mousetrap, spare rubber nose, telephone, several balloons, prop gun with spring out banner that says, "BANG," exploding cigar, giant pair of plastic scissors, rubber chicken, rubber ice cream cone, rubber hand, whoopee cushion, bag of confetti, fake cast, toy cannon ball marked "BOMB," and a pair of old socks between two slices of bread.

If you are a great comic acrobat like Fiveish the Clown you could even stash away in your deep clown pockets three raw eggs.

Fiveish dropped the eggs into the hat, quickly put it back on Izzy's head then sat on it.

Izzy looked at the audience with not a quiver on his face.

The audience exploded with laughter.

For those who have never pondered the various styles of comedy, the word "deadpan" means the lack of expression on the face. Sometimes a blank stare at the end of a piece of mischief is funnier than an emotional reaction. Since Izzy's face showed no emotion what so ever, he was a natural though unwitting deadpan comedian.

The clown jumped onto a flagpole protruding from the movie house. Around the flagpole he swung, flying off with a double flip. But the audience didn't even see him do it. Their attention was on Frankenstein. They laughed and laughed at the sight of Izzy looking at them with a blank stare and crushed eggs seeping out from under his hat.

Out of the blue came a voice from the audience.

"Hey, I know that clown. That's the clown the cops arrested!"

The line of costumed characters stopped laughing then stared at Fiveish.

The little kid from earlier in the day with his cream cheese and liquorish bagel stepped forward and grinned; his teeth still stained black.

"He must have escaped!" he yelled.

Blood oozed out from a gash on his clown face, sutured with hanging thread.

"Get him!" he screeched.

As quick as the snap of a finger the friendly gathering of scary looking clowns turned into a horrifying group of ferocious ones.

"Why are you looking at me like that?" shouted Fiveish

The sinister throng inched towards him.

"What do you want from me? Why do you want to hurt me?"

Little Liquorish Teeth yelled, "Get him by the nose!"

"But I am one of you!" shrieked Fiveish.

Then the horde of clowns charged.

"I'm in an alternate universe!" he cried. He spun around to get away.

A slice of pizza flew towards Fiveish. He ducked; it slapped Izzy square in the face; hung there for a moment then fell to the floor leaving two pieces of pepperoni stuck to his eyes like a pair of sunglasses.

A garbage can flew through the air with its contents spilling out. It missed Fiveish by an inch. Scattered across the sidewalk lay soggy French fries and rotten cheese, spoiled hamburgers and soggy peas, moldy bread and baby diapers, two broken windshield wipers, a curdled milkshake and dried out baloney, a greasy steak and macaroni. The putrid rubbish teemed with squirmy maggots.

"Izzy! Run!"

Clowns skidded on the hamburgers, French fries and baby diapers. They tripped over the steak and broken windshield wipers. They slid across the puddled milk shake and slimy maggots.

Fiveish tried to get away but the mad clowns quickly encircled him. From the center Fiveish yelled, "Clowns are supposed to be funny!"

He jumped onto the shoulders of a clown then hopped from clown head to clown head.

"Ouch! He knocked my wig off!"

"My nose, my nose! He kicked the clown nose off my face!"

"Grab his clown shoe! Hook his suspenders! Don't let him get away!" roared the crowd.

The movie theater door swung open.

"Okay everybody," said a friendly usher poking his head out for the first time, "hand me your tickets as you walk in. He had a smile on his face.

"Help!" screeched Fiveish.

The usher's smile quickly disappeared.

Now let's take a moment to ponder the plight of this poor usher. For a measly few dollars per hour his evenings are normally spent selling candy, popcorn and soft drinks to patrons who enjoy watching movies. He checks tickets for friendly customers and insures behavioral and cleanliness standards.

But the moment Fiveish ran past him into the theater his regular evening turned into a precarious situation of life and death.

The rabble of clowns stampeded through the door knocking the usher to the floor. Each clown shoe that stepped on his body and face had something gooey, gummy or smelly attached to the bottom of it.

"Get out of the way!" they snarled.

Tossed about like a babies limp toy, he was bruised, battered and had many stains of unknown origin soaking through his ushers uniform. If he knew that smashed maggot juice was one of those gooey substances he would have passed out immediately.

The usher rolled then crawled behind the concession counter where the other employees huddled in fright.

The mass of cackling clowns trampled their way through the lobby then into the theater.

"Where's that sad faced clown?" said one.

"There he is! Don't let him get away!"

Using two broken windshield wipers as a balancing pole, Fiveish made his way across a row of seat backs like a circus high wire walker.

A double cheeseburger with extra onions flew past his ear. A hotdog with mustard, relish and warm sauerkraut whizzed by. A giant sized soda with crushed ice passed overhead.

Then little Liquorish Face scooped up a week old fudge brownie from the filthy floor. His parents were very proud of their little rug rat, he was the star pitcher for the Wellcatch Oil Refinery little league team. The stale piece of cake fitted his hand perfectly and was as hard as a hard ball.

He pulled his arm back, lifted his leg with perfect technique then pitched the ball.

Fiveish heard a whistling sound then a dull "thump."

He was hit smack in the middle of the forehead. He blacked out and fell off of the theater chair.

"HOME RUN!" he yelled. "Hey where did he go?"

"Look under the seats!"

"Dudes, I think the movie's starting!"

The clowns stopped their antics for a moment to watch the opening scene:

A YOUNG LADY tosses and turns in her bed. A clown steps out from a dark closet. It creeps closer until it is only inches away from her face. It is Imp, with bleeding fangs and bloodshot eyes.

THE MOVIE THEATER became silent; not a wicked clown stirred.

WITH A CHILDISH giggle, Imp lightly brushes her nose with a rotten finger.

"Tickle, tickle."

She opens her eyes; they grow wide. She screams.

Imp lifts a rubber chicken high above his head then swings it down...

SUDDENLY, WITH A rip and a tear, Izzy crashed through the movie screen.

"Frankenstein just ruined the best part of the scene," cried several clowns with disappointment.

The curtain fell down, the remnants of the screen collapsed and the camera operator up above was so startled that he knocked over the projector. The film began to smolder then caught on fire. Soon flames moved through the theater like a whirlwind.

Climbing out from under one of the front seats Fiveish yelled out at the top of his lungs, "Run out through the back exits!"

A large welt was growing on his forehead.

He pushed, tugged and pulled frightened clowns that did not look so evil anymore out the back door.

"Izzy!" he shouted, "jump off the stage and run this way!"

But Izzy didn't move. He gazed at the blazing fire swirling up towards the ceiling.

"Izzy!"

Fiveish tried to run towards him but a tongue of fire lashed across his way.

"Fire, fire, fire," said Izzy. "Up, up, up."

Then Izzy's eyes became clear as a vision came to him from out of the blaze.

He saw a space ship hurtling towards the sky then explode into thousands of burning pieces. Then within the black smoke he saw an opening between the stars. Beyond he could see endless star filled horizons. His mind began to work like a mighty computer as complex mathematical calculations flashed across his vision. Secrets of the deep and dark became laughably simple to him.

The fire crept up onto the stage.

"I can see, I can see!" he cried out as he lifted his hands towards the beyond.

He no longer looked like Frankenstein; he no longer had a deadpan face. He was now Isadore Elsenplace, the young teen with a mind that could see across time and space.

Wild flames roared above and below him as Fiveish stood helpless and watched.

"Isadore!" screamed Fiveish, "Your mother Elsie is calling you!"

Izzy blinked.

"Mom?" he mumbled.

He felt the heat of the flames for the first time.

His coat caught fire, then his hat.

A shadow sprang from the side of the stage. It dove into Izzy and pushed him like a football player off the side than out through the exit.

Fiveish ran out to the parking lot behind the theater to behold the usher putting out the flames on Izzy's clothing.

"You're going to be okay friend," he said.

"I saw fire and shadow," whispered Izzy with a deadpan face. "Fire, fire, shadow, shadow."

Sirens could be heard in the distance.

"You'd better go before they get here."

"Thank you for saving his life," said Fiveish.

"What a crazy night," said the usher, "I've never seen clowns act that way before."

"Nor I," said the clown.

The two of them helped Izzy to his feet.

They turned to leave but then the clown stopped and looked back at the usher. The theater behind him was now completely engulfed in flames.

"Please, can you spare some change so that Frankenstein and I can get a bite to eat?"

Suddenly the clown experienced a moment of deja vu.

The French word means, "already seen." Those who have experienced the feeling describe it as an overwhelming sense of familiarity with something that shouldn't be familiar at all. Say, for example, you sit down to eat a falafel sandwich in a crowded restaurant, but as you bite into it, all of the components within, salad, green olives, roasted jalapeno peppers, coleslaw, sauerkraut, tahini, hummus and of course the falafel balls, fall onto your lap leaving a soggy mess. Suddenly it seems that you have had this exact experience before. Or perhaps you tumbled into quicksand. While being pulled under towards a very unpleasant demise you have the feeling that you've already experienced this very thing.

There was something about asking the usher for money that seemed like déjà vu.

The usher took out some cash from his wallet and handed it to the clown who turned then disappeared into the darkness with his big friend.

With their hearts pounding in their chest, sweat

beading down their cheeks and the smell of smoke on their clothing, they rushed to the grocery store just before closing. The clown bought a quart of milk, fruit and some bread and cheese. The lady at the cash register was wondering when the little fellow would return.

They ran through the snowy grass of a nearby park then sat next to a tree under the full moon. It was getting warmer outside and the snow was beginning to melt.

They ate and drank their fill and they were happy.

The food made them drowsy.

Izzy lay down on a nearby bench while the clown leaned against the tree.

"Clown?" said Izzy, whose eyelids struggled to remain open, "Feeling strange. Not supposed to be here. I was funny, funny, funny."

"Thank you for inviting me into your house," whispered the clown, who was being lulled asleep by the light breeze. "And thank you for the hot tea."

Izzy was already snoring like an accordion.

"Thank you for caring and being a friend."

The clown's eyes closed.

He lifted a hand up towards the stars for a moment. With a sleepy voice he whispered, "King Almar. The Troubadours."

Soon the clown was also snoring, but his snore sounded like a cement truck without a muffler.

Chapter Ten
The August Clown

I T WAS LATE morning. The clown lay at the base of
the tree trunk. The park was empty.
Izzy was nowhere to be seen.

Just to make sure, he reached up and squeezed his
nose.

"Still dreaming," he quietly said. "Is Izzy also just
a dream?"

He made his way downtown sneaking through
back streets and alleyways. Sometimes he hid behind
trees and bushes. He was a strange looking figure
always hiding in the shadows.

There was a crowd of people up ahead. The
clown climbed inside the bucket of an old abandoned
backhoe. He peeked his head out. People were laughing.

Leaving the backhoe to get a better view, Fiveish
slowly crept closer. Suddenly, there was an opening
in the crowd. He couldn't believe it; a clown was
performing in the center of laughing adults and
children.

It was a different kind of clown than he. It was
an August clown. This type of clown had no beard or

sad lips. This clown had a white face with bright colors around its eyes and cheeks. Its lips were blue, and it had bright red hair. The clown's costume was huge and baggy with stars of all colors.

The August clown performed face painting, juggling, animal balloons, magic tricks, unicycle and stilt walking. Jokes were sprinkled throughout the routine.

Fiveish the Clown was also capable of doing those things, but it was acrobatics that he truly loved. He could almost fly through the air, tumble and flip, crash and cause a huge commotion and he was an expert at funny pratfalls.

He never thought about it before, but now he realized that just like there are many types of people, there are also many types of clowns. There is the white-faced clown, the character clown, and the silent mime, each clown so different from the others yet so wonderful, beautiful and unique, just like people.

He wanted to meet this clown since it looked friendly. If he could talk to it, maybe it could help him.

When the show was over, the August clown started bringing its equipment to a van parked on the street. Fiveish quickly ran over to help.

He picked up its unicycle.

"Hey you! Put that down!" yelled the August clown.

Fiveish quickly laid it back down. He was scared.

"I, I'm very sorry. I wanted to help you."

The August clown looked at the sad-faced Tramp Clown. "That's okay; you can help."

Together they stuffed the equipment into the back of the van.

"So where are you from?" Asked the August clown.

"It's hard to explain," answered Fiveish. "And I am afraid to tell you about who or what I am."

The August clown opened the door to the driver's side, climbed in, sat on the driver's seat but let its legs hang over and out of the car.

"Don't worry," it said. "I can keep a secret."

The August clown grasped its nose, pulled, pulled harder then, "thwack," its nose peeled off.

Terrified by what he just saw, Fiveish tried to run but banged into the open door of the van.

"Ooof!" he said then fell to the floor.

The August clown smiled.

"You're pretty funny. Is that in your routine?"

Fiveish stood then continued to watch as the August clown reached for a box, pulled out a sponge, put some cream onto it then begin to wipe the makeup off its face.

Fiveish's eyes widened as the August clowns makeup became smeared. Streaks of white, black, red, blue and green flowed together into a frightening mass. The grotesque swirl of colors mingled together turning into a gray mask. Its true skin finally appeared.

Fiveish was horrified; he wanted to run and hide. But then he saw that there was a real person underneath the makeup.

"You're, you're not a clown," he said, feeling faint and dizzy.

"Hey you just insulted me!" it said as it pulled off its red wig. "I work very hard at my job. Do you know how long it took for me to learn all that stuff? It took a lot of practice to learn how to juggle, do magic, unicycle and everything else."

"I'm very sorry," said Fiveish. "I didn't mean what I meant to think. I mean, I didn't think what I meant to say. Um, say to think. Think to think…"

"It's okay. Don't worry about it. That was pretty funny too."

Fiveish looked at the clown that was no longer a clown. It was a girl, and she was beautiful.

Tears started to form in the clown's eyes.

"I didn't mean to hurt your feelings clown," she said with gentleness in her voice. "Are you all right?"

"I'm fine," he answered. "But for a moment I thought that I was no longer alone. I thought that there were more like me. I thought that you were like me, a real clown."

"There you go again insulting me," she said. "I am a real clown!"

She closed the door to the van, disappearing from view. In a few minutes, she was back out dressed like a regular person. Her hair was blondish red and pulled into a ponytail. Her face was clear from all makeup, but she looked a little tired from the hard work she put into her clown act.

She saw that the Tramp clown was still hanging around.

"How can I help you clown?"

"Pull my nose," he said.

"Okay, now your freaking me out," she said. "Should I call the police?"

Then Fiveish reached up and pulled his nose. He pulled with all his strength.

She looked at the struggling clown oddly for a moment. She reached into her van then pulled out a sponge.

"Stop moving!" she said as she tried to remove his makeup. She scrubbed at it really hard, but the makeup did not come off.

"This isn't makeup, it's more like a tattoo!" she said with astonishment. "Who did this to you. If it's a practical joke, it's not funny!"

"I can't remove my clown shoes either, they're stuck to my feet," he said.

"Somebody put super glue into your shoes?" she gasped. "How awful!"

"And my body is bent, and my legs are bowed," he whimpered. "What has happened to me? I am alone in the world."

She stood there quietly, not knowing what to make of him or what to do. She reached her hand out and hesitantly patted his shoulder.

"You are not alone," she said. "I will help you. Get into the van."

As they drove together through the crowded city streets, Fiveish kept looking over at the girl. She was the first human to really try and help him with his problem. Even Izzy couldn't help him.

"Human?" he thought. "If she is human then I am a freak, a creature."

"Thank you for trying to help me," he said.

"That is what clowns are for, to cause smiles. So let's see it, let's see the smile. Come on."

But he couldn't; he was afraid of what was coming up, afraid of the unknown.

The clown looked out the window. There seemed to be millions of people moving all about like ants.

"What am I?" he asked.

"Don't worry," she answered. "Where we are going, they'll be able to figure out everything."

"And besides," she said, "If you think you are having a bad day, just imagine what I went through the day before yesterday. My show was completely ruined by this rude guy in a black suit and bowtie."

The floodgates were opened. The memories began to pour into his brain. He saw the juggler, the slack rope walker and yes, even the white face clown.

His eyes widened then he turned his clown face away in shame.

The truth of what he was began to dawn on him. He was horrified and disgusted with himself. It was terrible what he had done to this clown, this beautiful person.

"Are you all right?" she asked.

But he did not answer. He could not speak.

Something else began to dawn on him, something unspeakably horrible. Since the girl sitting next to him remembered her show being ruined, which took place before his nightmare began, didn't that mean this terrible adventure that he was stuck in was actually real and not a nightmare at all?

"No, no, please no!" he whispered.

"Don't be afraid," she said. "We're here."

She parked the van.

"Let's go."

The little clown closed the van door then looked across the street. There it was, the hospital. Ambulances parked in front, nurses, doctors and patients walked in and out of the doors. The building was massive. The clown gazed at the modern edifice that seemed to reach up to the clouds.

They walked through the hospital door together but were stopped by a tall security guard.

"Whom are you visiting?" he asked.

"This little guy is the talent," said the girl.

He looked down at the clown.

"I know you," he said. "I saw you on instagram yesterday."

They started through the door, but they were stopped again.

Looking down at the girl, he said, "And who are you?

"I'm the talent agent," she answered with an over zealous smile.

"Okay, go ahead in."

Holding the clown's hand, she guided him across

the tile floor, past a beautiful fountain and a statue of a surgeon with a clown face holding a circular saw.

"Why would they have such a frightening sculpture here!" asked the shaking clown.

But when he looked again, he saw to his relief that it was only a normal doctor and the saw was really only a ball that he was handing over to a young child.

"Am I going mad?" he asked to nobody but himself.

"Okay, see over there?" she said pointing. "That's the nurse's desk. They'll help you. Go ahead. You're going to be fine now. Good luck clown."

"Good-by," he said, with a heavy heart.

He slowly walked towards the reception desk, but then stopped short, turned around and ran back to the girl.

"Don't be afraid," she said with a soft voice and gentle smile. "You're going to be fine."

"It's not that," he said. "I have been hiding something from you. I am the man in the black suit and bow tie. It was I. I ruined your show. And I have also hurt many others. I am no good. I am evil."

The girl stood there silently for a moment pondering what was just said.

"Listen," she said. "People change. You have obviously changed. There's a reason for what's happening to you."

She stopped for a moment then looked deeply into his big clown eyes.

"I think that you are a good person. You don't realize it, but you have actually helped me. The day before yesterday I was... I think this is a quote from you: "Just a clown that walks around blowing up balloons!"

She put her hand on his clown cheek.

"You were right," she said with tenderness, "that is all I was. At first, I was devastated. I cried and moaned. I felt like an untalented nobody and was ready to quit it all and go back to being a court stenographer. But I didn't give up. I rethought my whole act and brushed up on the other clown arts. I researched the history of clowns and how they developed through the ages even from ancient times. I changed my costume and makeup and made changes to my clown character. I stopped just doing balloons. Instead, I used my balloons along with jokes, tricks, and funny buffoonery. I was up all night making big changes. You saw it today. It's not perfect yet, but it has opened a whole new world for me. You have opened a whole new world for me."

She stopped for a moment, took a deep breath then reached over and kissed the clown on the cheek.

"Thank you," she said. "I want you to know that you have changed my life. Now go! Go get help from that nurse over there that is sitting at her reception desk."

He turned with a renewed smile on his sad clown face and walked in the direction of the nurse's desk. There was a feeling of hope starting to build up inside of him.

Chapter Eleven
Doctor Rancid

"EXCUSE ME; I need to see a Doctor."

The nurse looked at the clown then said, "The children's ward is down the hall. Turn left then take the elevator to the fourth floor."

"No, I need to see a Doctor," he repeated.

"I said the fourth floor!"

He turned then walked down the hall.

The elevator door opened. He stepped in but just before it closed a doctor and a nurse quickly slipped in.

"Here is the medical chart you asked me for Doctor Rancid," said the nurse.

"It is about time," he snarled.

Doctor Rancid wore a white lab coat and had a stethoscope hanging around his neck. He wore round sunglasses. He had a scraggly black beard that stuck straight out from his chin. His skin was white, his hair black and the shape of his head was long, kind of like a football.

"And what is that perfume emanating from you? It's turning my stomach."

"I'm sorry Doctor," she replied.

"Is that a coffee stain on the chart?" he asked. "Do you know how unprofessional that is?"

"I'll make sure to be more careful," she said as she lowered her head in embarrassment.

"Do my eyes deceive me? No, they do not! Your name badge is slanting! Not good, not good.

"I, I'm sorry Doctor Rancid, I..." she could not finish for tears burst forth from her eyes.

"Your tears will not help you, young lady," he said. "Take my learned advice and quit your job. Try basket weaving."

The doctor noticed the clown for the first time.

He smiled with an unfriendly smile then said to the young nurse, "No, I have a better idea for you. Learn to become a clown. Yes, I think that would fit you very well."

He looked into the clown's eyes then said, "Don't you think she would be just great as a clown? I think that she should enroll in Clown College and get a degree in clowning. Clown College is in Florida is it not? Why yes it is. She should move to Florida right away; she shouldn't wait."

He brought his face close to the clowns.

"Well, what do you think clown?"

The little clown looked at Doctor Rancid; then he looked at the young nurse who was bent over with tears. Doctor Rancid reminded him of someone, but he couldn't quite remember whom and he didn't want to think about it.

He gulped then said, "I think that you are a very mean and cruel doctor."

The elevator door opened then Doctor Rancid stepped out and walked away chuckling as he went.

The little clown patted the sad nurse on the shoulder as the elevator door closed.

"It will be okay," he said. "I think that you would be a great clown." But that only made her cry even more.

"Oops, sorry, oh boy," he said. "What I meant to say was that I could teach you to be a clown."

But her sobs just worsened.

"I know, I know, that was also the wrong thing to say. Holy mackerel!"

The elevator door opened.

"Can you show me the way to the children's ward?" asked the clown.

That did it. The nurse wiped her eyes with a tissue, straightened herself up, smiled then said, "Right this way Mr. Clown."

Just in case you did not catch that, the nurse stopped her tears only after the clown asked her where the children's ward was; in other words he asked her for help. This is an example of a universal truth: helping others can destroy sadness. By doing a good deed, by helping others or by giving charity, pain can turn into comfort; sadness can turn into happiness, poverty can turn into wealth and darkness can turn into light, not just for the receiver but also even more for the giver.

"There's the entrance to the children's ward Mister Clown," she said with a smile.

Fiveish the clown ran down the hall then skidded on his big clown shoes through the doorway and across the floor of the children's ward.

Standing between several hospital beds, the clown bowed elegantly then pulled a flower from his sleeve, brought it up to his red clown nose then sniffed a big sniff. A fly flew out of the flower then shot straight up his nose.

Now, for those of you who don't know about this, Fiveish the clown was a master of pantomime, ventriloquism and goofy sounds. So, when the fly quickly found its way into his clown nostril, the children believed that it was a real fly.

The clown shook, squirmed, spun and flopped around as if the fly were caught in his red clown appendage.

Then the clown stopped moving. He quietly looked at the children. He suddenly covered his nose with a paper bag, bent his head back then threw it forward.

"Ha-ha-ha chooo!"

The fly shot out of his nose and into the paper sack.

"Ha-ha! I caught ya!"

Suddenly the bag, coming to life, pulled him to the left then pulled him to the right. When it pulled him to the left again, the clown fell on his chest. It slid him across the tile floor.

The children were going insane with laughter. And

the young nurse from the elevator was holding her stomach and chuckling.

The clown stood up, but the fly in the paper sack yanked him, and then yanked him again. It became a game of clown-fly tug-o-war. Back and forth they strained. The fly was winning.

The children's laughter caught the attention of the hospital security guards. With hands on guns, they began to creep closer.

Without warning the fly in its brown paper bag flew between the clowns legs, pulling him upside down or downside up or inside out or outside in. Whichever one it was, the poor clown flipped over then found himself flat on his back.

Fiveish became worried; the children's faces turned red from their manic laughter. Their eyes seemed to bulge.

Nurse's, doctor's, visitors and other patients from different parts of the hospital joined the audience. He became frightened when he saw how crazed their laughter was.

"This is not normal," he mumbled.

The security guards were not laughing.

He quickly brought the show to an end. Bowing to the children, he carefully made his exit past the security guard with a fake smile and a wave.

The young nurse caught up with him.

"Thank you Mister Clown; I have never laughed so hard in my life."

Now out of sight, he ran down the hallway turned

Frank Michael Adams

a corner then crashed into a doctor. They both fell to the floor.

"Hey, be careful!" said the doctor, standing then brushing himself off. His nametag said, "Doctor Dubin."

"You can't stop clowning around can you clown?" he said. "I saw you in there with the children. It's great what you do, visiting people when they're sick. But I think you do more then that; you give them the healing power of laughter. I hope you come again."

The elevator door opened and Doctor Rancid stepped out. As he passed by Doctor Dubin and the clown, he said, "Clown school is in Florida Doctor Dubin. I think you would be much better off over there with your own kind."

Doctor Dubin wisely refrained from answering him back, but wondered what he meant by, "own kind."

Impatiently the clown said, "Listen Doc I have a problem. Pull on my nose."

Something about this conversation made Doctor Rancid curious. He stepped around a corner hiding from their view then quietly listened.

Doctor Dubin laughed then said, "You're kidding right?" He slowly reached over and gave a gentle tug on the little clown's nose.

"Harder!" cried the clown.

He gave a harder tug.

"Ouch! You see, I can't get my nose off my face! I can't get my face off my face; it's stuck! I thought it was a dream, maybe it is, I don't know anymore! I'm going crazy, Doc! Please, you've gotta help me!"

The doctor just stared in amazement.

"It's a trick," he said. "It can't be."

He slowly reached out his trembling hand then squeezed the clown's nose really hard. The loud horn-like squeak from the red nose caused the doctor to jump back and almost fall into a medicine cart.

"Follow me!"

He led the clown to an examination room, not knowing that Rancid was following closely behind. He sat the clown down on an examination table.

"Wait right here. I'm going to try and find another doctor, a specialist who might be able to help you. Don't move!"

He quickly ran out the door and then down the hall.

Rancid looked both ways to make sure that nobody was around. He quickly stepped into the room that the clown was waiting in. He grabbed the little clown by his shirt then pulled him into a different examination room.

"I am the specialist that Doctor Dubin went to find."

"That was fast," said the clown.

Then he realized that this doctor was none other then the dreadful Doctor Rancid.

"No! It can't be," cried the poor little clown.

"Let me look at you. How strange, I've never seen anything like it before. I think we have a rare specimen here. I don't think there is another one like you in the entire world. I'll be rich!"

Startled, the clown said, "What?"

"I mean, I'll be richly interested in finding a cure for you. But first, you'll need a shot."

"A sh-sh-shot?" whimpered the clown.

The menacing Doctor Rancid pulled out a long needle then walked towards the frightened clown.

"Wait Doc, you forgot something; you forgot to tap my knee."

"Why yes, of course, you are right," he said grinning. "How silly of me. Doctors always tap knees, don't they?"

He pulled out a small rubber hammer and gave the clown a light tap on the knee.

Like lightning, the little clown's large clown foot sprang up by reflex and kicked the doctor in the nose. He went tumbling across the room and fell backward over a chair. When he sat up, his stethoscope was dangling from his ear.

The clown ran through the door as fast as he could while shouting, "HELP!"

The clown ran down the hospital hallway. He didn't notice the "DANGER WET!" sign posted next to a puddle of spilled orange juice. At full speed, he ran through the juice, slid with his feet along the hallway then crashed onto a hospital gurney.

The bed with wheels rolled down the hallway then down a flight of stairs hitting the wall at the bottom.

The poor clown flew off the gurney then into a laundry chute.

"Help!" he yelled as he shot down the slippery shoot winding every which way. The echo of his helpless voice got weaker and weaker the further down he slid until no sound could be heard at all.

At the end of the chute, he was flung into the air across the hospital basement like a wet noodle.

His clown shoe knocked a mop out of its stinky bucket.

He rocketed through the open door of the laundry dryer.

The smelly mop bounced off of a sheeted cadaver, flipped several times in the air then tapped the dryer door shut.

The smelly mop which at this point seemed to be more then just an ordinary mop, landed perfectly balanced on the tip of its handle. Fiveish watched in horror as it slowly fell over hitting the button marked "ON".

Just a moment, please! It is important to remember that this unlucky clown was a profoundly advanced acrobat. Fiveish the comic acrobat was trained by the great Mark Hundi, who was trained by the great Kazamatsu, who was trained by the great Shinsu, who was trained by the great Watanabi, who was trained by Gordon W. Patuski who was known to be the world's fattest acrobat and broke the Genus Book of World Records for the most corpulant person of all time to do the quadruple back flip.

Diving through hoops on fire or lined with razor

blades is one thing but even Fiveish the Clown was surprised by the impossible stunt that he just completed. Even the mighty King Flatimus of ancient yore could never, in his wildest imaginings, dream of pulling off a stunt like that!

Yet here he was.

The dryer machine began to turn. It spun faster and faster while the sad clown looked out with his sad face through the sad glass. The world turned around and around while he helplessly watched the villainous Doctor Rancid step down the stairs towards him.

Normally it would be an act of kindness to save a pour soul trapped in a hot spinning laundry dryer. But there was no kindness in Doctor Rancid's inner being.

He pushed the stop button. The clown fell to the bottom of the machine like a limp towel. When he opened the door of the dryer, the clown tumbled to the basement floor.

Doctor Rancid and his long needle were ready for him.

"No," said the clown.

Ten seconds later he was sound asleep.

Chapter Twelve
The Operating Theater

IN TIME, THE clown's eyes fluttered open. The world seemed foggy and distorted, colors blurred into each other.

"Where am I?"

Images began to materialize.

"Is there a show starting?" he asked to no one.

A small theater quickly filled with people. He tried to sit up then realized that he was strapped to a gurney.

Fear began to well up inside of him, and he felt his blood fill with adrenaline.

Adrenaline is an almost magical substance that can give people almost superhuman powers. The body produces it only when experiencing great and sudden fear, like the clown was experiencing at that exact moment. But alas even with this almost magical substance flowing through his clown veins, he was still not able to break the tight straps holding him down to the hospital gurney.

He was now fully awake.

A man walked to the center of the stage then spoke into a microphone.

"Wait a minute!" the clown thought.

The truth was beginning to dawn on him.

"That man isn't dressed like a ringmaster; he's wearing a white lab coat."

Suddenly, he knew where he was. He was still in the hospital, and this wasn't an ordinary theater where people go to enjoy a musical production or ballet, it was the operating theater in the hospital. And that wasn't an ordinary audience; it was an audience of doctors, nurses, and scientists. And all of them were wearing white lab coats.

My friends, just in case you do not know what an operating theater is, I am compelled at this time to tell you.

An operating theater is where medical students watch from seats in a small auditorium while a doctor who is a specialist, performs a unique, rare or very complicated surgical procedure.

But there were no medical students in this audience.

He realized that this clown show was not going to be an ordinary clown show, certainly not the type where the clown just walks around blowing up balloons. He was trapped in a very unordinary clown show, a wake up screaming clown show. And that wasn't just a doctor, it was...

Ladies and gentleman, boys and girls, if you have ever had a nightmare that was really bad, not just bad but really, really bad, then you might know just how scared the little clown was. It was none other than the diabolical Doctor Rancid. The scared little fella was really in trouble now.

Rancid began to speak:

"Ladies and gentlemen, doctors, scientists and professors, you have come from far and wide, traveled on short notice from different parts of the globe, some by plane, some by train and even one by hot air balloon, to see a wonder, a unique phenomenon reveal itself before your very eyes. You are about to see a medical discovery that will turn anthropology upside down and cause human evolution to be rethought. It is now time for you to witness this historic marvel."

The audience was full of anticipation.

"What could this mysterious thing be?" they quietly mumbled.

"And now, what you've all been waiting for, the one, the only, the incredible, Fiveish the Clown!"

There was silence. The audience was confused. Did he say, clown? Their eyes were glued to the stage.

Blank faced interns slowly rolled the hospital gurney with the odd creature bound to it towards the middle of the stage.

"Unfasten him," commanded Rancid.

Slowly the small goofy looking character with a sad face and a red shiny nose stood up then rubbed its wrists. The interns held it tightly then forced it to hobble over to the side of Doctor Rancid. The eyes of the fascinating creature were tightly shut, and it was shaking uncontrollably from fear.

The audience seemed to hold its breath from excitement.

The strange bent thing with big feet stood there quaking.

The clown slowly opened its eyes. When he saw the audience, he let out a loud squeak, jumped in the air then crashed onto the floor. Frightened like a scared bunny rabbit, he quickly sprung up and ran off stage.

The audience was not expecting this and nearly hit the ceiling when the clown squeaked. After a moment, they began to laugh.

Doctor Rancid and an intern picked up the little specimen by its arms and carried him back to the middle of the stage with his clown feet kicking the air.

"Ouch! Leave me alone! You're hurting me!"

"Quiet!" said Rancid.

The audience was now in an uproar of laughter.

The doctor, now angry, stepped to the microphone.

"Stop laughing!" he demanded. "This isn't funny; this is serious. This isn't a clown show! You ought to be ashamed of yourselves."

He looked out into the audience then said gravely, "You are among the greatest scientific minds in the world and look how you are acting while this extraordinary event is about to unfold before your very eyes."

The audience became quiet, except for a few giggles here and there.

"Come here clown," ordered Rancid.

Fiveish slowly walked over to the doctor.

"Now, be a nice little clown and give me your nose."

Fiveish looked at the doctor with pleading eyes and pointed to his nose.

The doctor nodded with a yes.

The clown looked at the audience then gulped. He slowly brought his big shiny red nose close to the doctor.

"Ladies and Gentlemen," said Rancid with a smile, "notice the red, bulbous proboscis. The bone is formed in such a way that if you squeeze it, it makes a musical note. Observe."

Rancid snapped on light blue rubber gloves then reached over and squeezed the clown's nose.

It honked.

Again the audience laughed.

"Silence!" he commanded. "Stop laughing, this is not funny, this is not a joke! Esteemed doctors and scientists, this is not just a person with make-up on and a rubber nose; this ladies and gentlemen is a real clown, perhaps the only one like him in the world. Witness!"

He pulled forcefully on the clown's nose, trying to show the audience that it was a real nose.

"Ouch, that hurt!" yelped the clown.

The audience was now rolling in the aisles.

"Stop laughing!" Rancid cried. "He's real I tell you! You must believe me!"

He gave another tug on the clown's nose. Then from his pocket he retrieved a scalpel.

"Behold!"

Now dear readers, especially the very little ones, it is important for you to know what exactly is a scalpel. There are many types of knives in the world. Some are made for cutting vegetables, some for cutting steak, some for cutting through a thickly tangled jungle and others used to defend oneself from an attacking bear. None of those are very useful for a doctor. But every doctor owns a scalpel. It is an extremely useful tool for surgical operations such as removing large unsightly moles or clown noses. Though the scalpel is much smaller than a machete, it is a frightening thing to look upon. Though many people have been helped and even saved by this unique blade, I do not think that there is a medical patient in the entire world who is not frightened by the sight of a brightly polished scalpel.

The little clown looked at his reflection in the scalpels cold steel.

It suddenly dawned on him that in Rancid's opinion he was not a human being at all. Rancid considered the little clown only a thing, a creature like a fetal pig, lab mouse, experimental rat, frog or Rhesus Monkey, ready for dissection with his shiny razor sharp scalpel.

The clown needed to take action right away.

Fiveish, no longer Mister Nice Clown, and remembering what he did to police officer Dooley, lifted his big clown foot and stomped down onto the toes of Doctor Rancid.

"Ouch!"

And as he began to hop around on one foot, the audience began to clap and laugh out loud.

Rancid, who's face had now turned as red as the clown's nose, began to chase the little fellow around the stage.

Just at the moment Rancid was about to grab him, and remembering his expertise at Parkour, the clown ran two steps up the wall and flipped backward over the doctor's head. While the clown was still in the air, the dastardly doctor ran under him and slammed into the wall with a loud "bonk." The little clown landed right behind the doctor, and then with his floppy shoe, gave him a big kick in the caboose.

Rancid turned and tripped over the clown's feet, fell head first into a waste paper basket where his head remained stuck like a cork. He stood then ran around bumping into chairs and walls. He finally fell onto the very same hospital gurney that the clown had previously been strapped to.

The big interns tightly secured the raging Doctor Rancid onto the gurney.

Fiveish quickly put on a white lab coat that was so big it dragged on the floor.

"Can opener!" yelled the clown.

Doctor Dubin who had just rushed into the operating theater stopped, looked at the turn of events then handed him a can opener.

Now you may be wondering what in the world Dr. Dubin was doing at that moment with a can opener? Well if you were close enough to him to smell his breath, which is something that I really do not recommend you do, you would have smelled the distinct odor of tuna fish. After gagging a bit, you would realize that Dr. Dubin had just finished eating a tuna fish sandwich. The can opener for the tuna was still in his hand when he heard loud banging and crashing coming from the operating theater.

Using the can opener, the clown opened the side

of the waste paper basket. Doctor Rancid's face poked out.

"Feather!" yelled the clown.

Doctor Dubin handed him a large feather.

You may also be wondering what Doctor Dubin was doing with a large feather? He was a Taxidermist by hobby. Taxidermists enjoy stuffing animals, usually animals that they themselves have hunted. Hanging from office walls, placed on a shelf behind a desk or stuck in a dusty corner somewhere, one may find a Marlin, a Grizzly Bear or a Bald Eagle forever mummified in time like a statue at the very moment before their life source suddenly terminated.

Moments before eating his tuna sandwich, Doctor Dubin glued a large feather to his prized stuffed vulture. But it didn't stick. It actually fell onto his open fish sandwich. Thus when he heard the boom and bang coming from upstairs, he had also just taken a bite out of his tuna fish and vulture feather sandwich.

It is a wondrous thing how the secret power permeating the universe, sets in motion an unlimited host of occurrences that ripple and vibrate in mysterious ways to bring about awesome events, great achievements, extraordinary solutions or a filthy scavengers quill right when they are supposed to happen.

"Koochie, woochie," said the clown, as he began to tickle Rancid's nose with the feather.

The audience, by this time, was laughing so hard that tears were streaming down their cheeks, and their bellies were beginning to ache.

"Shoe!" roared the little clown.

While coughing up vulture fluff, Doctor Dubin removed the shoe from Rancid's foot.

"No, please," begged Rancid, "not that, anything but that!"

"Now the sock," said the clown with a rascally smile.

Dubin removed it then held his nose while waving the sock in the air.

The clown tickled Rancid's malodorous foot. He squealed with laughter even louder than the audience. Tears squeezed out of his eyes then streamed down his cheeks.

The three big interns with white lab coats, had now become turncoats by helping the clown. They wheeled Rancid away while he laughed like a hyena.

"That was a very entertaining show," said an Infectious Disease Specialist. "But what was the occasion?"

"Ah Wunderbar! What a great hospital this is," said a Psychiatrist with a thick German accent. "They put on shows for their employees to help release their stress levels."

"I'd like to stick my p-p-probes into that l-l-loony doctor's brain," said a Neurologist unbuttoning then re-buttoning his shirt for the twenty-third time.

The clown turned and said, "Thank you very much, you've been a wonderful audience. It was so kind of you to travel from far and wide just to see my little performance. I hope you enjoyed it. Thank you. Good day."

There was a large applause then the curtain closed.

The lights faded while the doctors and scientists exited the operating theater.

The clown was alone on stage. He stared at the empty theater in front of him.

Memories began flooding back into his mind. Strange ghostlike images began to swirl in a spiral around the theater. He saw the images of a penniless flower peddler and a man asking for charity. He saw lonely children in hospital beds. He saw a ruined juggler and a muddy slackline walker. He saw a lonely tattered man sitting in a lonely cardboard castle. And then he saw an august clown remove its clown wig revealing a beautiful girl with reddish blond hair and a lovely smile.

Tears came to the clown's eyes.

"What sadness," he whispered to the empty theater. "There is so much sadness. There is so much…"

The clown became dizzy, and the room began to spin. Everything seemed to turn into a psychedelic blur. The clown collapsed onto his knees then fell forward to the floor and then there was only darkness.

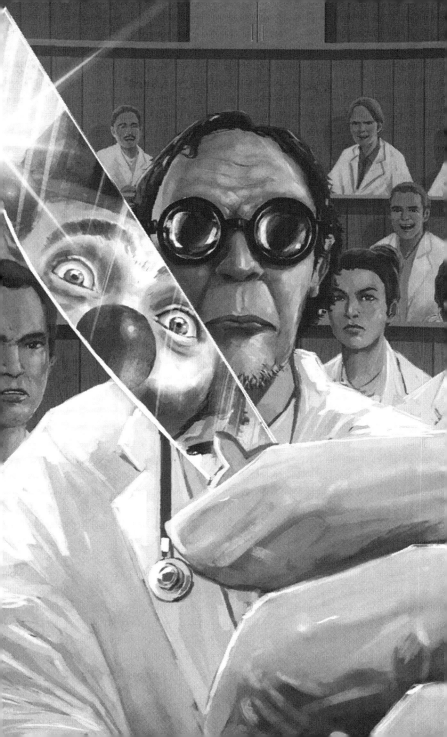

Chapter Thirteen
Dancing in the Street

"Up! Wake up Fiveish! Fiveish wake up!" Someone was shaking him. He opened his eyes, sat up and looked around. He was on the stage floor of the Mystique Theater with the closed curtain in front of him.

"Are you okay, Fiveish?" said the Stagehand. You passed out. We were worried about you."

"It's you Mr. Stagehand," he said. "I think I had a dream or nightmare or… I'm not sure! Can you do me a favor? Can you pull on my nose?"

The Stagehand looked at him strangely but slowly reached over and gave a pull.

It was on the tight side; Fiveish really had put too much spirit gum on it, but finally it gave and the nose pulled off with a loud "thwack."

The Ringmaster stood back a bit in the shadows watching. He tapped his tophat with his fingertips as if he were rapping on a Bongo drumb. He watched as the clown stood then made his way to the side of the stage.

The clown ran along the hallway then turned into his dressing room. Sitting in front of his makeup mirror, he looked at his reflection. He wiped his face with a towel and some cream. Looking down at the towel, he saw that it had a large streak of black, white and red grease paint on it.

"My face is coming off!" he yelled out happily. "My face is coming off!"

The people outside his door heard this and thought that Fiveish was going a little coo coo.

"Oh! Thank you, thank you!" His eyes became wet with tears as he danced circles in his room.

He quickly dressed into his street clothes and then ran down the hall towards the stage.

"My face is coming off," he said, quickly passing the stagehand.

"My face is coming off," he said with a crazed laugh to the curtain man as he skipped along.

"My face is coming off," he said while doing a round off back handspring past the sound technician.

He turned then ran across the stage to its edge then flipped off it landing in the carpeted aisle.

He ran through the lobby, through the decorated double doors then outside into the night.

The Ringmaster, watching him go, had a far away look on his face. He put the top hat back on his head then tilted it just right. He looked at the large paintings decorating the theater walls. He smiled. With the monocle on his eye and his lifted eyebrow, he quickly turned and walked away into the shadows of the Mystique Theater.

What a peculiar sight he was, running through the

streets, stopping people on the road and shouting, "My face is back!" Most people were frightened of him; you see he had only taken off half of his makeup. Imagine being stopped by a crazy looking guy with half of a smeared clown face.

A four-year-old girl holding her mother's hand while walking along the sidewalk spotted Fiveish.

"Look, Mommy, a clown, a funny clown."

But when Fiveish slowly turned showing the other half of his face, the smeared messy side, the child cried, "Scary clown! Bad clown! Go away clown!"

The mother lifted her arm then swung her purse hitting the half clown on the head.

She dialed 911.

"911 dispatch," said the dispatcher.

"A raving madman is threatening my child," said the mother.

Fortunately, the half clown half man was already far away singing and dancing in the street.

"He-he-he, ho-ho-ho and ha-ha-ha-ha-ha," he sang while dancing like a ballerina on his tippy toes. He jumped and spun in the air like a monkey and he did back handsprings across the street. Several cars skidded to a stop trying to avoid hitting the happy creature of the night.

"Hey! Get out of the street you crazy lune!"

The full moon was getting low. It looked like it was filled with air like one of the clown's giant balloons. It hovered like a white blob above the dark horizon. The strange silhouette of the man with the half clown face could be seen dancing and spinning in front of it. When the Moon finally set, the frolicing silhouette vanished with it into the night.

Chapter Fourteen
In Search of Answers

L ATER IN THE night Fiveish the Man awoke from sleep. His heart was thumping, his hair sweaty and his shirt damp. Something was bothering him. He laid his head back on the pillow but tossed and turned; sleep was impossible. Chucking the tangled sheet off the bed, he rose to his feet.

He sauntered into the kitchen. There was a chill in the air. After making a mug of hot chocolate, he leaned back on his recliner. Reaching out and turning on the lamp next to him, he remembered another time where he was cold, and a steaming hot beverage, a soft chair, and a bright lamp cheered him up, and this was not Deja vu.

"Izzy!" he whispered. "Are you real? Do you exist? Or was it really just a dream after all?"

He tried to see the August clown in his mind. He tried to see her lovely face, but it was growing dim.

"I need to remember you," he whispered. "Don't leave me."

But her image faded into a misty blur.

After he finished his mug, he went back to bed. He laid his head down and in moments was back asleep.

Late that morning after a small breakfast, he left his apartment determined to get to the Mystique Theater as quickly as possible.

He took the train into the city. When he got off, he saw the very same man in rags that he saw near the subway or L-train that asked him for charity the other day. After taking out his wallet, he walked up to him.

"Don't hurt me," whimpered the ragged person who was frightened of Fiveish the Man. "I don't want your money. You were mean to me."

"I am sorry that I acted that way to you," said Fiveish. "Please forgive me. I will never act that way again. What is your name?"

"Bob, my name is Bob."

"Here Bob, please take this."

He placed a bundle of cash into his hands.

"I'll come by and visit you again to see how you're doing."

Fiveish turned to go then stopped.

"Bob, do you know anyone by the name of Izzy or Isador?"

"No," he answered."

"Good-by for now," said Fiveish.

He made his way along the crowded street. He saw things that were familiar to him but never thought about. Everything looked different. He saw poor people, men and women wearing tattered clothing who were hungry and sad. It broke his heart. Why had it not broken his heart before?

He crossed the street while dodging taxies and a garbage truck. And then, "bang!" he bumped into the flower peddler. Both of them fell to the sidewalk. The flowers were strewn all about.

He helped the flower lady back onto her feet.

"I'm not selling any flowers to you, mister," she said. "You're a person who hates beautiful and delicate things."

"Yes, you are right to say that to me," said Fiveish, "I truly apologize."

He reached into his wallet and pulled out a hundred dollar bill then handed it to her.

I don't have enough change to break that size bill," she said. "Do you have anything smaller?"

No, I don't, said Fiveish as he handed her another hundred dollar bill and then another.

"You see, I want to buy them all."

From the ground he lifted the scattered bouquets and single flowers.

"I have scarcely pondered the beauty of a flower."

The flower peddler saw deep sadness in his eyes. She put her hand on his shoulder.

"It seems to me," she said, "that something odd has happened to you, mister."

"Something has."

He pushed his nose into the load of flowers and breathed in deeply. He giggled for a moment when he thought about the fly and the paper bag.

"Thank you," he said. "Do you know someone by the name of Isador Elsanplace, also known as Izzy?"

"Can't say that I have." She answered.

He turned then ran in the direction of the Mystique Theater.

He stopped for a moment, looking to his right. Was it a driveway or a street? He wasn't sure, but something about this place was important; something happened here.

Crossing the street, he ran up the concrete steps then into the theater.

There was a buzz of activity. Stagehands were setting up scenery, and lighting men were putting up colorful lights. He ran backstage and there they were, the boys who tried to help him with his costume and suitcase the other day. When they saw him, they backed away.

"Don't worry," he said, "I want to give these to you."

He handed each of them a bouquet of flowers. He turned and ran down the hall. Up ahead was the stage manager.

"This is for you," he said.

The stage manager hesitantly snatched it from his hands.

With a great pile of flowers bulging in his arms, he hurried from makeup designer to costume designer, set designer to lighting designer, special effect person to curtain man, music director to prop man, electrician to janitor and all the actors, singers and dancer in the theater. He gave them all flowers. Then he ran up to the director of the theater.

"This is for you sir."

"Thank you," he said nervously. "Should I get you a psychiatrist?"

"Where is the Ringmaster?" asked Fiveish.

"He'll be by later in the day," he answered.

But he was there, hidden and watching. From the interior of his top hat emanated a purple glow.

With the flowers that were left in his arms, he ran out of the theater and into the street. He gave flower after flower to one pedestrian after the other until only a small bouquet was left.

He rushed down the narrow alleyway to the back of the theater while his chest heaved in and out with each breath. When he reached the back door of the theater, he stopped. He looked left then right. There was the garbage can he remembered from the dream or episode, which he was now beginning to call it. A cat bounded out of it and away when he approached. Trash and debris were scattered about. There was the same dumpster further down the alley, but only bags of rubbish lay within.

There was no dead catamaran and no decomposed car with its guts hanging out. The lone cardboard box next to the cinderblock wall was gone. He walked up to the wall then examined the blacktop at its base.

"No entrance of anything," he whispered.

He climbed to the top of the wall then looked over to the other side, again nothing.

The junkyard observatory with the lush greenhouse within was gone. The big old telescope that pointed towards the sky was gone. And the cardboard castle was nowhere to be seen.

"Where did everything go?"

From atop the wall Fiveish looked out at the city skyline across the river. The Oakenstock Bridge spanned the waterway bustling with ocean freighters coming into port from far away places.

Jumping down from the wall he returned to the steps by the theaters back door. He sat then lifted his eyes upward towards the sky. With all the power he could muster from his lungs he called out, "Izzy!"

But there was no reply.

~

HIS NEXT STOP was the park. He spotted the broken down backhoe, walked past it to the place she did her performance. He felt a sense of desperation growing inside of him. He looked out at the children playing on the slide and merry-go-round. He wanted to see her again; he needed to see her again before she was gone from his mind forever. He looked for her van by the street. The August Clown had disappeared from his life.

"I never even knew your name."

He hailed a taxi, but when the driver saw that he was the same dude who threw the money in his face, he quickly drove away.

"Creepo!" he yelled out of his window.

The next taxi took him to the hospital.

He asked the nurse, "Does Doctor Dubin work here?"

She answered, "There is no Doctor Dubin in this hospital."

Hesitating for a moment, he asked, "What about Doctor Rancid?"

The nurse suddenly stiffened.

"There used to be a Doctor here by that name. He has not been back to this hospital for many years."

"But I saw him here yesterday."

The nurse seemed frightened.

"Where did he go?" asked Fiveish.

"The story that I heard was that he went on a long trip, but no body knows where."

When Fiveish turned to leave, he heard the nurse whisper under her breath, "Thank God."

His next stop was the police station. He asked the sergeant, "May I speak to police officer Dooley?"

"Let's see," responded the sergeant. "Yes, he is here in the station today. I'll page him."

Fiveish was hopeful.

In a few minutes the police officer arrived. But it was not officer Dooley; it was an officer by the name of Daily.

It was getting late, and Fiveish was tired. He sat down on a park bench. He looked at the trees. The snow was long gone and the grass was freshly raked from old autumn leaves, the smell tickled his nose.

Then he remembered something. This was the same bench that Izzy slept on that fateful night.

He looked out at the buildings along the street. There was the grocery store where he bought milk. A few blocks down would be the bank where the police arrested him. A light wave of fear lingered at the memory of it. Next to the bank was the library.

"Hmm, is it possible?"

FIVEISH STEPPED THROUGH the sliding glass door and into the library. It was stifling hot inside.

With the computer, he searched for the name Isador Elsenplace, but there was nothing. He typed in the words: WORM-HOLE TO OUTER SPACE, EASY CONSTRUCTION USING SIMPLE HOUSEHOLD MATERIALS, but again nothing.

Then he went to the newspaper section and asked the librarian for the old newspaper archives.

"These archives are still in microfilm," she said. We haven't converted it to digital yet."

"That's okay," said Fiveish as he sat at the console punching in the name Isador Elsenplace.

He searched back through the years, each year giving no results until he reached 1972. Suddenly there he was. Fiveish was staring at a photo of Izzy! Even then he had that same emotionless face, that deadpan face.

The headline in the Collywobble Review stated:

23-YEAR-OLD MAN MYSTERIOUSLY DISAPPEARS, WITNESSES SAY, INTO SPACE!

THE ARTICLE READ:

"Isador Elsenplace, the talented child genius that dazzled his home town by memorizing the entire encyclopedia word for word, mastered seventy languages and easily understood abstract math and physics, wanted to remain with his friends in high school rather than be the only 14-year-old at the University. On his first day of school as a freshman, during his first history class, during the first minute of class, a bully pushed him. He fell backward through a second-floor window. He suffered a fractured skull and brain damage. He was never the same.

Doctors stated at the time that while he grows into an adult, his mind would remain like a child's.

Then two days ago, twenty-three-year-old Isador Elsenplace, known by his friends as Izzy, suddenly disappeared.

Witnesses testified that he shot into space from a roller-coaster rocket that detached from its track at a locale amusement theme park where he and his questionable younger friends secretly spent the night. The fiery tail of the rocket capsule could be seen miles away and by hundreds of people as it streaked across the night sky then into space.

Isador Elsenplace has not been seen since."

"But I have seen him," thought Fiveish.

Chapter Fifteen
The Traveling Clown

MANY YEARS WENT by. Fiveish the Clowns antics had been seen across the globe. He was hailed as the King of Comedy in such places as Paris, England, Berlin, and Splitzelglattin. He performed in front of the great King Slawswalski. He was given the prized Golden Clown Shoe of the S.O.C., the Secret Organization of Clowns.

These days, most of his shows are for charitable purposes.

He did a show in Brazil, raising a very large sum of money to help save the rain forest. The friendly natives even cleared a large swath of ancient, delicate and rare jungle trees to accommodate his large stage.

He did a show in the war-torn valley of Kam San Tu to help bring peace to the devastated area.

The Fighting Klan of the Renubi tribe loved his performance and laughed till tears were brought to their eyes. The Brotherhood of the Foo Koo Rami Dynasty screamed with delight as they watched the little fellow crash and fall in the most hilarious ways. The clown even brought up two high-ranking members of these sworn enemies as volunteers. They laughed and had wonderful fun together as if they were children.

When the show was over there was great applause. The clown was lifted into the air by both factions then swooshed away to his van, which quickly drove out of the mountains.

Thus, began the final battle of the Valley of Kam San Tu. There were hardly any survivors, but they laughed until the very end.

AFTER FINISHING HIS Irish scone and tea, Fiveish the man straightened his black bow tie then headed out the front door. But before closing it he stopped, turned around then looked back inside.

On the wall were two paintings. On the left was Fiveish the man with a clenched fist and a scowl on his face. To the right was a duplicate of the first, only the hand was relaxed and lifted as if he were giving something away. And the face had a friendly smile.

He now had many visitors and guests. Many thought it strange to have paintings like that next to each other. But to Fiveish the man, it was an important reminder of who he was and what he could become.

He was not yet ready to think that he was truly changed. It was possible that he could still lose himself and go back to the monstrous thing that lurked inside of him and lurks inside all of us.

But that strange place he once visited and the strange adventure he had afterwords changed him somehow. It was a place where the laughter was just a little too loud, and his jokes just a little too funny and the audience just a little too, well, loony.

He smiled then locked the door.

He jumped onto a bus, which brought him to the subway, which brought him to the airport. The plane flew across the country then across the ocean landing on an airstrip near the foot of Mount Babagwa, its sharp peak still filled with snow in the higher altitude.

On yet another bus, he traveled across the countryside then up into a high mountain village where a black limo waited for him.

The limo brought him up a steep road through a mysterious looking old growth forest. A decorated iron gate opened in front of them. A winding driveway brought him up up up to the entrance of one of the most beautiful and majestic resorts in the world, "The Resort in the Sky."

"Your bags are waiting for you in your changing room sir," said the doorman.

"Thank you Sisk," said Fiveish the Man as he handed him a generous tip.

He rang the bell at the concierge station.

"Good evening sir," said the concierge. "Step right this way, and I'll show you to your changing room."

"First I must see the stage," said Fiveish.

The concierge led the way.

"Good, the clown suitcase, the ladder, and the table are all in the right places.

"Shall I show you to your changing room now sir?"

"Thank you yes," answered Fiveish.

But then he stopped and looked up. Though this was a wonderful resort, its stage was not really meant for a show such as Fiveish the Clowns. A giant chandelier hung from the ceiling right above his mini-trampoline.

"Wow! That could have been a problem," he said.

He adjusted the mini-tramp and safety cushion to the side just enough so the chandelier was out of his way.

He looked at the concierge, smiled then said, "To the changing room!"

With another friendly tip and a light bow, Fiveish said, "Thank you," to the concierge then closed the door.

He was alone.

He sat at the makeup table with the round mirror and its lights. He looked at his face for a moment then opened his dented makeup box. He took out a tube of white grease paint and was just about to start on his lips when the door squeaked open behind him.

Through the reflection in his mirror he saw somebody slowly sneak up towards him.

He quickly stood up and turned around. His eyes widened at what he saw, but then a smile engulfed his face.

"My August clown," he gently said.

"My Sad Faced Tramp clown," she replied with a lovely smile.

They embraced then looked deeply into each other's eyes.

"I looked for you," she said, but I couldn't find you

anywhere. You were gone from my life as if you never existed. I thought that I would never see you again."

"And I looked for you," he said with deep tenderness. But I thought that you were only the beautiful part of a very long dream."

She touched his face.

"It isn't a dream; it can't be," she said. "If it was then how is it possible that I have looked for you all these years?"

"And if it was a dream," he said, "how is it that you are here with me touching my face?"

He caressed her hand that was on his cheek.

"You're real," he said with tenderness, "you're real."

There was a knock at the door.

"You've got 15 minutes Fiveish!"

"Wait for me at the end of the performance," she said. "I have something important to tell you."

She quickly left Fiveish's dressing room.

He took a deep breath. He felt like the world was tilting again. It seemed that reality and illusion were mixing together like an abstract oil painting, or like his face when he smeared his makeup.

"What is happening to me?" he asked his mirror. "Am I here? Am I in Clown Alley? Or am I in both worlds? What is going on?"

But when he thought of her face, he smiled and relaxed.

"She is back," he thought. "She has come back to me."

He quickly put his clown nose and makeup on, next was his costume. The last things he put on were his clown shoes.

He ran to the side of the stage and waited for the Ringmaster to announce him.

The music for the previous act just ended. With his black tuxedo and cape, a magician bowed deeply, turned then walked off stage. He passed the clown, but as he did so he bumped into his shoulder then quickly walked away.

The music started for the clown show. Fiveish hurried on. But as soon as he entered the stage, he slipped on something greasy, flew up into the air then landed flat on his back.

The audience reacted with a huge explosion of laughter. The laughter turned to giggles. The giggles turned to silence when they realized that the clown was not moving.

The Ringmaster and the Stage Hand quickly ran to the clown.

"My back," he said with difficulty. "I can't move."

The Ring Master and Stage Hand looked at each other; there was concern on their faces.

With help from the theater nurse, they lifted the clown onto a stretcher; he grimaced in pain.

"Ha-ha-ha!" laughed a single audience member realizing that this was all just part of the act. Unfortunately for him, he quickly found out with embarrassment that it was definitely not all part of the act. The audience member sunk deeper into his chair.

They lifted up the stretcher then brought the clown off the stage.

"That fall was not part of my act," said Fiveish, his voice weak.

Every breath brought stabbing pain to his back and ribs. He was carefully brought to his dressing room. They gently laid the stretcher down onto the couch.

"Somebody spread a puddle of oil on the stage," said Fiveish, "and I slipped on it.

"A doctor's been called," said the Stage Hand.

Fiveish tried to get up, but the pain was too much for him.

"Stay down," said the Ring Master, "you may have injured your spine."

"I need to get up," said the clown pitifully. His pain could be seen through his colorful grease paint.

"The show must go on!" he cried.

"Not this time my friend," said the Ringmaster, who was handed a slip of paper from the hallway.

He read it then stepped out of the room.

"Just rest now," he said before closing the door behind him.

With the note in hand, the Ringmaster quickly walked back to the middle of the stage then faced the audience.

"Ladies and gentleman, boys and girls," he belted out, "a slight variation has been made in the sequence of acts this evening. So without further ado, please welcome, the one, the only, Atzmo the Clown!"

The members of the audience looked at each other

and mumbled. They wanted Fiveish the Clown, but they also knew that he was hurt. They decided to give this newcomer a chance.

A sad-faced tramp clown ran on stage.

He began to juggle balls. He was quite good. He climbed up Fiveish's ladder then toppled over it, landing on the stage floor.

Some of the audience members giggled.

MEANWHILE, THE DOCTOR arrived. He stepped into the changing room. His face was covered with a hospital mask and his eyes were hidden behind thick sunglasses. He immediately put a hot compress on the clown's eyes and forehead, blocking his vision.

BACK ON STAGE, Atzmo stepped into Fiveish's metal bucket then clanked around the stage.

There was silence from the audience.

He brought up a volunteer. She pulled off the bucket then went back to her seat.

The audience began to mumble.

"This guy is trying to steal Fiveish's act!" said a lady in the first row.

"HURRY UP, GET me some paper towels!" ordered the doctor.

"Right away," said the Stagehand.

As soon as he was gone, the doctor pulled out from his pocket a shiny scalpel.

ATZMO THE CLOWN jumped up onto Fiveish's table then back flipped off.

The audience was beginning to get upset.

THE DOCTOR SLOWLY crept towards the clown with the scalpel held out in front of him. The sharp blade glistened as it moved closer and closer to the clown's throat.

The door suddenly swung open.

"Here are the paper towels," said the stagehand breathlessly.

The doctor quickly pulled away from the clown then hid his scalpel.

Fiveish could hear what was happening on stage through a speaker hanging on the changing room wall.

One person in the audience loudly said, "Get off the stage you bum!"

He heard another say, "We want Fiveish the Clown!"

Then he heard Atzmo say back to the audience, "Ah shut up!"

Fiveish got up on his elbow.

"I have to get out there," he said.

He rolled off the couch then onto his knees.

"What are you doing?" said the stagehand.

"That's right," said the doctor, "you can't just get up and run around in your condition. You must rest."

"Those are children with cancer out there in the auditorium," uttered Fiveish. "You have to help me get out there!"

"But your hurt!" said the Stagehand.

"This is absolutely ridiculous," said the agitated doctor.

"Some of those kids won't last a month!" said Fiveish the Clown, gritting his teeth.

The stagehand helped him to his feet. The clown was sweating from the pain. Holding tight, they made their way out of the changing room, the Stagehand on one side of him, the doctor on the other side.

While moving towards the stage, Fiveish could see Atzmo's performance from the side.

Atzmo adjusted the mini-tramp to the center of the stage. Then went around and adjusted the safety cushion.

"No!" said Fiveish.

"Do you think Fiveish the Clown will mind if I use his mini-trampoline?" asked Atzmo.

"Boo!" was heard from the audience.

"You have to stop him," yelled Fiveish. "No!"

Atzmo backed up then began his run towards the tramp.

Fiveish reached the side of the stage then yelled, "Stop!"

But it was too late.

Atzmo hit the mini-trampoline at full speed right in its sweet spot. He flew high through the air like a beautiful swan then crashed into the giant chandelier. He sliced through thousands of glass diamonds and hundreds of light bulbs. The chandelier shattered. Glass rained down onto the stage and across the auditorium. There were shards of sharp glass on the floor, on the seats and upon the heads and shoulders of the audience. They sat in silence as the powdery dust that was contained within the bulbs floated down like a light snow. There was a whimper from an elderly man. Then there was a feeble cry from a young child. Then the floodgates were opened. There was uproar of screaming, crying and shouting as the audience stood then stampeded out of the auditorium in a complete and sudden panic.

Fiveish tried to climb off the stage to go and help the frightened people but he couldn't. He fell into the arms of the stagehand and doctor.

"They're going to be alright," said the Stagehand. "The nurse and the theater crew know what to do to help."

Fiveish, the stagehand and the doctor walked to the center of the stage, their feet crunching bright colored glass as they went.

Atzmo was on his knees holding his ears. Glass and glass dust were tangled within his clown wig.

"You're in big trouble fella," said the stagehand.

But Fiveish touched the stagehands shoulder silencing him.

"Are you okay?" asked Fiveish.

But Atzmo's eyes were tightly closed. A small bead of blood dripped down his forehead then onto his clown nose.

The audience had gathered in the lobby.

Fiveish the Clown turned to see the maintenance crew with several large vacuum cleaners come in and begin their business. When he turned back, Atzmo the Clown was gone, and the doctor was nowhere to be seen.

But the audience in the lobby saw them. The doctor was chasing after Atzmo while repeatedly hitting him on the head with his cane. He chased him out through the big resort doors.

The Ringmaster, looking carefully at Fiveish, asked, "What do you think?"

With a painful smile, the clown answered, "The show must go on. Let's do it!"

Through a loudspeaker, the Ringmaster blurted out, "Ladies and gentleman, boys and girls, the theater has been cleared of all debris and is now safe to re-enter. Fiveish the Clown has recovered and will start his performance in five minutes.

The audience nervously re-entered the auditorium then took their seats.

"The Ringmaster stepped to the center stage then said, "Is it Oneish?

"No!" said the children.

"Is it Twoish?"

"No!" said the children with the adults.

"Is it Threeish?"

"No!" said the mothers and fathers.

"Is it Fourish?"

"No!" said all the boys and girls.

"Well, then what time is it?"

"It's Fiveish!" shouted the entire audience in a cheering uproar. The Ringmaster, stagehand and curtain man cheered. The nurse, light technician and set designer cheered. The maintenance men, plumber and sound technician cheered. And a beautiful girl with reddish blond hair also cheered with happy tears in her eyes.

Fiveish walked out on stage, looked at the audience, waved to them then smiled. They responded with applause.

He walked up to his mini-trampoline then looked at the chandelier, half of it was still hanging from the ceiling. He re-adjusted the position of the mini-tramp and safety cushion then stepped back to the beginning of the runway at the side of the stage. He looked at the audience again just for a moment then rubbed his aching back.

The audience understood then laughed out loud.

He backed up another step then began his run.

The audience was worried, many of them tightly clutching their seats.

The clown sped down the runway, jumped onto the trampoline at full speed then took off like a missile, flew through the air much higher than the chandelier. The audience saw the clown through the remaining glass diamonds and bulbs while he did a full twist at the apex of his dive. It all seemed magical. The colors of the diamonds reflected blue, green and yellow off the clown's costume. It looked like it was in slow motion. He exited from behind the chandelier then landed safely onto the safety cushion.

Fiveish stood up then lifted his hands into the air like a champion.

The audience rose up and cheered until their throats were sore.

"We knew you could do it Fiveish," yelled a parent.

But actually, for a moment, they weren't so sure until he landed safely. Sighs of relief could be heard coming from the audience.

Even though his technique was off because of his back injury and he wasn't able to do even a tenth of what he was capable of doing, it did not matter. The chandelier dive broke the ice, no pun intended.

The audience laughed at everything.

If he raised his index finger, they laughed; if he sneezed, they laughed; if he crossed his eyes, they laughed; if he picked up his foot and wiggled it, they laughed; even if he said "Poo-poo," they laughed and laughed.

Fiveish the Clown was back.

Even before the show was over, newsmen and women were on their cell phones texting, tweeting, face booking, instagramming, snapchatting and emailing the newspaper headlines.

The Collywobble Review was already being printed; it said:

"FIVEISH THE CLOWN SAVES THE DAY!"

The Bloviate News, which was just rolling off the press, said:

"CLOWN BACK FROM THE DEAD!"

The Codswallop Examiner blogged:

"TO BE OR NOT TO BE... TO BE!"

The Slangwhanger post tweeted:

"THE HEALING ANTICS OF A CLOWN!"

After the show he hobbled back to his dressing room with the help of the stagehand. He stepped through the door and saw her. She stood in front of him looking at his face.

"My sad little clown," she said.

She ran up to him, grabbed his suspenders then kissed him. Black, white and red grease paint now colored her lips and cheeks.

Before the clown could recover, she said, "Hurry,

we have to go! Take your makeup off then get into your street clothes fast."

"I don't understand," he said confused. "What is the rush?"

"Please trust me," she said. "I'll wait outside the door for you. But please Fiveish, hurry!"

Chapter Sixteen
On the Run Again

FIVEISH OPENED THE dressing room door. She was waiting for him.

"Hurry!" she exclaimed

Taking his hand, she led him to the edge of the stage. Before jumping he stopped, sat down on the edge, slowly slid his way to the ground then rubbed his back.

"Come," she said.

She pulled him into the auditorium. They ran up the aisle into the lobby, out the large resort doors, down the steps then into the waiting black limo.

"To the airport," she commanded the chauffeur.

Startled, Fiveish said, "What?"

"Don't worry," she said, trying to calm him. "Your luggage and gear is being stowed."

"But what is this all about?" he asked.

"Please darling, trust me just a little longer."

A bullet hit the limo near the back window missing Fiveish by inches. The projectile bored through the back seat then lodged itself into the trunk.

The squealing of the tires blocked out the sound of the guns discharge. He had no idea how close he was to death.

THE AIRCRAFT MOVED smoothly through the air high above the patchy clouds. Fiveish's head leaned against a porthole window; he was sound asleep. The snowy mountains were far behind while the wide ocean lay ahead to the horizon.

She laid her head upon his shoulder but remained alert.

The stewardess pushed a beverage cart along the isle.

"Would you like something to drink Sir," she asked a gentleman in a gray suit.

But he did not respond.

As she passed him by he rose from his seat then made his way towards the front of the jet.

Lifting her head from Fiveish's shoulder, she observed the gray suited man.

"What would you like to drink today Mam?" asked the stewardess to a woman with so much make-up on that she looked a bit like a clown.

"Do you have pickle juice?" she asked.

"We have orange juice and apple juice."

"How's about goats milk?"

"We have soda, seltzer, water, scalding tea and searing hot coffee."

The jet abruptly swerved to the right. The

stewardess fell sideways onto the lap of Prince Walywaly. Her serving tray toppled over and its contents flew sideways. The searing hot coffee splashed onto the prince's hands.

The plane swerved to the left. Luggage flew out of their overhead compartments and the passengers began to scream.

Fiveish remained peacefully asleep.

She disengaged her seat belt.

The plane rapidly took a dive. The stewardess tumbled down the isle with the heavy beverage cart following close behind.

Then the plane began to climb steeply, its jet engines shrieked.

Using the seats like rungs on a ladder, she inched her way like a mountain climber towards the cockpit.

Most passengers, not having time to buckle their seatbelts, held onto the seatbacks above them for their lives.

Garbage, laptops, purses and food filled the open space inside the jet.

Reaching the cabin door she supported herself by tightly holding onto the door brace. Swiveling sideways, she lifted her knee then broke the door open with an odd looking sidekick.

The pilot was unconscious while the copilot was being strangled.

She jumped onto the back of the gray suited man, got her hooks in, (in Jujitsu lingo, getting your "hooks in" means that your legs circle around the opponents body while your feet tightly wrap inside the legs) then quickly pressed her thumb into the pressure point at the base of the skull. The ancient martial art technique is called the "Touch of Death" or in Cantonese, "Dim Mak." It is often referred to as "the evil twin of Acupuncture."

But before he was put to sleep the muzzle of his Ruger 380 small handgun pressed into her armpit.

She released her thumb from the pressure point then began to back away.

The gray suited man smile then cocked his gun.

Just a side note: There are certain places in this world where a gun should never be cocked. One should never cock a gun on a submarine, zeppelin, police headquarters, space station, or in front of a faster draw then you, and never ever cock a gun in a pressurized jet cabin two miles above the earth.

But stuff happens in the heat of the moment.

There was suddenly the sound of a vibrating whistle.

The thug in the gray suit went limp then fell to the floor unconscious.

The copilot quickly regained control of the aircraft.

Prince Walywaly stepped into the cockpit; lifted his homemade boomerang from the floor, pulled four more of them from under his vest then proceeded to juggle the five boomerangs together. They spun hypnotically in the air creating wind like a fan even with the second-degree burn on his hand.

"A direct hit," she said.

"At your service my love," said the prince.

Prince Walywaly, known as just Waly to his friends, was a man of many talents. He was the direct descendant of King Lamalama of the heroic Dingy-dingy Dynasty. He was 7-time winner of the World Wakabunga Outback Kangaroo Racing Championships, the all time Extreme Boomerang Throwing Champion, an ominous bodyguard and an amazing chauffeur.

After securing the goon, they made their way back to their seats.

"He sleeps like a babe in arms," said Wally wrapping his injured hand.

"Yea," she said, "he's cute that way isn't he?"

WHEN THE PLANE landed, the rush was on again.

When they exited the terminal, another black limo was waiting for them. They climbed into the back seat with Waly behind the wheel.

THE LIMO PULLED up to the front of the Mystique Theater; Fiveish had not seen it in years.

"There's no time to waste," she said. "We must get into the theater at once."

They ran up the steps to the entrance of the old opera house, but the doors were locked. She looked back and saw five men stepping out of a blue car across the street.

Waly stepped out of his limo, took aim, drew his arm back then threw his boomerang. The unusual projectile made a wide curve through the air. It went in one window of the blue car and out the other window. It pinged off the skulls of two thugs, dropping them to the pavement.

"That was a good shot, if I do say so myself," said Waly, who then crumpled to the floor after being hit with a Taser.

"This way," she said, pushing Fiveish along.

They ran around the side of the theater then down the alley. Memories started to flood into Fiveish's mind again. When they reached the dumpster, they stopped.

"Help me."

They leaned onto the dumpster, pushing it to the side.

To Fiveish's surprise, he was looking down into the darkness of Izzy's trap door. He looked back towards the street before he ducked under the surface. Three men quickly entered the alley then started to run towards them.

After pulling a lever the dumpster moved back to its place covering them from the outside.

Down they went, but instead of going towards the place where Izzy's cardboard castle once was, they turned towards the theater. They came up inside of a closet in a dressing room. They ran into the auditorium then along the plush aisle, up the very wide ornate stairs to the mezzanine.

The place was in shambles. The great paintings were all gone, dusty cobwebs hung from everywhere, gaping wounds showed on every wall, the carpet was burned and the once beautiful stage curtain hung in tattered strings.

Running up the winding staircase to the upper balcony floor, she led him into one of the private opera balconies.

She pulled back one of the stained tapestries. A small metal door was revealed.

"Give me your bowtie," she said.

"What?"

She removed it from his neck then extracted a small piece of paper hidden inside the knot.

"What are you doing with my bowtie?"

She handed Fiveish an eyepiece.

"Read what it say's."

"*Drab as a fool, aloof as a bard,*" he recited.

"What kind of code is that? A three year old can figure that one out. Read it backwards."

He slowly read it backwards.

"Drab as a fool, aloof as a bard."

"You see? It's the same thing. It's a palindrome, the simplest code to break. There must be something else to it."

Fiveish coughed.

"Ah, no there is nothing else to it," he said.

"What do you mean? Do you know how to decipher codes?"

"That is not a code."

"Not a code, then what is it?"

"It's a Chinese fortune cookie note," he said with some embarrassment. "The bow tie is a very convenient place to stash my favorite ones."

Exasperated, she said, "I thought I knew everything about you."

"Hey, I'm not the one sneaking secret messages into peoples bowties," he said.

"There has to be another message in here."

She probed deeper into the knot.

"Ah here it is. Read this one."

She handed him the small slip of paper.

"It say's, *FXJAJSWYBTQSNSJW.*"

"It's a Monoalphabetic Cipher!" she blurted. "Let's see."

She pulled an odd saucer shaped gadget from her coat pocket.

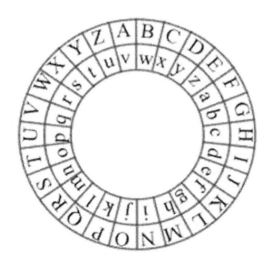

This," she said, "is an Alberti Disc. What is the first letter?"

"F," he replied.

She turned the inner disc so that its letter "A" lined up with the "F".

"Now that the disc is set we simply match up the code letter on the outer disc with the alphabet letter on the inner disc."

Fiveish read off the coded letters again while she wrote down the translation.

"Here it is," she said. "*SEVENRTWOLSIXR.*"

She circled the R, L and R.

"There you have it, *SEVEN RIGHT TWO LEFT SIX RIGHT.*"

Using the code, she quickly unlocked the metal door then squeaked it open.

I think dear readers that a long overdue explanation is in order.

This beautiful young lady, whom I am sure you have come to understand is much more then just an August Clown, was also the master of over two thousand codes and ciphers, a renowned safe cracker and a black belt in Brazilian Jujitsu, Muai Thai, Catch Wrestling, Northern and Southern style Kung Fu, Jeet Koon Do and Fisticuffs.

If one were able to examine her deep and hidden pockets without getting their lights knocked out, one would find more bizarre gizmos then clowns have.

One would find a disguise kit with fake glasses and three different colored wigs, invisible ink, very sharp set of throwing knives, poison hair pin, miniature telescope, brass knuckles, mouth guard, smoke bomb, set of 25 different lock picks and a whole slew of code breaking devices like the Polybius Checkerboard, the Skytel cylinder, the Thomas Jefferson Wheel Cipher, a miniaturized Enigma Machine, a Code Maker Slide Ruler and a Swedish Trans vertex HC-9 Cypher Unit. But her golden prize, the code-breaking unit that she never parted with and would protect with her very life, was the Andromeda 5 Intergalactic Alien Decoding Device, invented by our dear friend Issador Elsenplace.

"Hurry, step inside! That took far too much time."

"Now can you tell me what is going on?" asked Fiveish. "I think you need to explain this to me."

"Please Fiveish, you need to trust me."

"You've said that over and over again," he replied with frustration. "I know that we are being followed, but why?"

He stepped into the hole in the wall then she followed. She closed the door, which put them into complete darkness.

"Hold my hand," she said.

She felt along the wall, found an old rusty handle.

"Help me."

Together they were able to push the lever up. A large metal door opened. There was a faint light within.

"Come."

She closed the door then pushed down on the lever. The small room started to descend.

"An elevator!" said Fiveish.

"Quiet!"

Down and down they went. When it finally stopped, she opened the door.

"We are in the underground catacombs below the old opera house," she said. "Let's keep moving."

"Wait a minute!" said Fiveish. "I've been very patient darling, but that kiss you gave me only goes so far."

"Okay," she said. "I think we are safe for the moment."

"Safe from what?"

"Fiveish," she said, looking at him directly in the eyes. "You are in grave danger. That accident you had on stage was no accident. Someone is trying to kill you."

"What!" he said with a voice that was just a little too loud.

"While you slept on the flight, there was an attempt to take control of the aircraft."

A splash was heard off in the distance.

"Put this on," she said.

From an opening in the wall, she lifted two spelunking lanterns. Fiveish had never seen one of them before. It was a hard hat meant for cave exploration with a liquid gas torch attached to the top.

She pulled out a lighter, turned a knob on the hard hat then lit the lantern. A bright flame lit up the tunnel. She then lit her own lantern.

"Please hurry," she pleaded, "They are almost upon us."

"Who are you?" asked Fiveish.

"Not now," she responded.

They ran along a winding tunnel. Footsteps could now be heard off in the distance.

"I've been here before," said Fiveish, as he remembered from long ago the dark passage to Clown Alley

Their feet sloshed in the murky water as they ran.

She suddenly came to a stop.

"What is that?" she cried.

A monster tractor tire blocked their way. It went from one wall to the next and was wedged in like a cork.

Whoever was chasing them, they were now splashing through the dirty water close by.

"That wasn't here before," she said, "We're trapped!

"Wait. I can get to the top," said Fiveish.

He squatted and tried to jump expecting to do what only Fiveish the Clown can do but searing hot pain shot through his spine. He fell to the ground.

"Let me try," she said. "You'll need to help me to the top if you're able."

Fiveish lifted her as well as he could. When she made it to the top, she said, "Your turn."

He was leaning against the black rubber of the giant tractor tire, grimacing from pain.

"Grab my foot and climb," she said. "Please, you can do it!"

With her help, he finally made it to the top.

"Well clown," someone said from the shadows. "We finally meet again."

Into the lantern light stepped the magician whose act was right before Fiveish's. He wore a black tuxedo and cape with a black magicians hat. His sidekick Atzmo the Clown was at his left along with three tuff-looking hoodlums at his right.

"Who are you and what do you want with me?" asked Fiveish.

"Oh, that is a long story," he answered, "too long I am afraid to finish with anything but a fast if sad ending for you."

The girl took off her hard hat then unscrewed from it a threaded plug. She began pouring the liquid kerosene all around the top of the giant rubber tire.

"What have I done to you?" asked Fiveish.

"Well let's see," he said.

He lifted his white-gloved hand then began to count with one finger at a time.

"One," he said, "you didn't break your lousy clown back when you slipped on my invisible oil."

"Two, I was stopped in your changing room from slitting your clown throat by your clueless stagehand."

"Three, the idiot clown standing next to me tried to ruin your act by doing everything you do but before you did it. Instead, he made you even more famous!"

"Why do you want to hurt me?"

Atzmo laughed out loud. The magician hit him on the head with his cane. Atzmo's laugh quickly died as he rubbed the top of his skull.

"Why I am not going to hurt you," said the smiling magician, "I am going to kill you."

"I don't understand!" yelled Fiveish.

"Maybe you will understand now," said the magician.

He stepped into the very center of the light, took off his magician's top hat, put on his sunglasses then bowed.

"Is it all becoming clearer to you, clown?" he said with a smirk.

Fiveish's eyes widened.

"Rancid!" he said.

"Yours truly, but it's Doctor Rancid. You ruined my career. You embarrassed me, made a mockery of me in front of my colleagues and an international contingent of doctors, specialists and scientists. Kill him!"

His goons ran towards the tractor tire.

The girl reached down with her lighter then lit the tire on fire.

"Jump Fiveish!" she screamed.

The two of them leaped down the other side of the tractor tire to the wet cement below. She landed on her feet, but Fiveish was rolling on the ground in pain.

She helped him up.

"Go, go, go," she stuttered.

They ran away from the flaming tire as fast as they could. The fire scorched the top of the tunnel with black soot.

"Get them!" screamed Rancid.

"We can't boss, the flames are too high."

"Get them anyway, or I'll throw you into the flames myself."

Smoke billowed outward from the tractor tire. Soon, the tunnel was engulfed with choking fumes. Rancid and his henchmen retreated.

The black smoke began filling the tunnel.

On the street above, black pillars of smoke curled into the sky from storm drains and sewer lids.

The two of them ran as fast as they could but the smoke gave chase. In moments rubber-burning smoke caught up to them. They were engulfed by it then began choking.

They stopped, tried to hold their breath but couldn't. There was nowhere to go. It was over.

They could not see each other for the smoke was too thick, but they embraced.

"I'm sorry Fiveish," she said as the smoke choked her lungs. "My sweet, sad-faced clown.

They fell to their knees.

"My August Clown," he said.

They brought their lips together, staying that way until unconsciousness overwhelmed them. They fell to the floor still holding each other.

Chapter Seventeen
The Magical Center Ring

IVEISH AWOKE INSIDE a dark tent. His throat burned; it was difficult for him to swallow. While rising to his feet, a twinge of pain shot up his back. He threw open the tent flap. Colorful rays of light shot in. The interior of the tent lit up like a rainbow aquarium. She lay on a mattress at the other end. He sat by her side.

She was beautiful as she slept. He touched her hair. Her eyes fluttered open. Smiling, she sat up then took his hands. Rising to their feet, they walked out of the tent.

Blue clouds rushed by. The sky between the clouds was like the breathing sea covered in rainbow oil.

Circus tents surrounded them, the color of the rising sun.

"Follow me," she said.

They slowly walked beyond the circle of tents. Then there she was, standing by her tent flap, the gypsy from long ago. She no longer beckoned him to enter. With a far away look, she gazed at them as they passed.

A colossal circus tent loomed before them like

a mountain. It was decorated with shooting stars of every color. And diamonds, rubies and other priceless stones seemed to rain down. The tent changed colors as they approached. It flickered with every step.

They went inside. It was a one-ring circus.

Acrobats swung back and forth on the trapeze while performers of every type rehearsed their skills.

When the trapeze artists saw them, they stopped swinging, stood on their high platforms then waved to them far below.

A family of high-wire walkers balancing in a pyramid, one on top of the other, patiently made their way across the thin ribbon high above the circus net. When they reached the end and rested in safety, holding onto the support, they waved down at the newcomers.

A cannon of awesome size stood near the side of the tent. It was covered in chrome and shiny like a mirror. The Human Cannonball sat with rag in hand massaging oil into its mechanical parts.

"Welcome," he said.

A tumbling acrobat flipped off his ladder, landed on a teeterboard, springing his partner high into the air.

After landing on his friend's shoulders, they said in unison, "Hello Fiveish."

"Greetings," said a lone unicyclist while he rocked back and forth to keep his balance.

"Nice to see you Fiveish," said a stilt walker polishing the metal parts of his stilts.

Four jugglers were tidying up their rings, clubs, and

balls as well as props of every variety. Three of them said, "Hey it's Fiveish the Clown!"

One of them walked over to him then said, "Do you recognize me mate?"

"Is that you Waly?"

But seeing him in his juggling costume brought back an embarrassing memory.

Waly was the juggler whose show Fiveish the Man had ruined.

Fiveish blushed then said, "Yes, that was a long time ago. I'm very sorry."

"No worries mate. He's been waiting for you. He's over there sitting on the bleachers."

The Ring Master rose to his feet then stepped down from the stadium seats. His top hat had just the right tilt. He gingerly tapped it with his fingers tips.

"You're looking quite chipper today," he said with his mischievous smile. "We almost lost the two of you."

"Where is Doctor Rancid?" inquired Fiveish.

The Ringmaster looked at the girl who suddenly turned her face away. There was something troubling her. He gently put his hand on her shoulder.

"Rancid," said the Ringmaster as he let out a deep sigh, "he is a tragic one, a sad story. He's out there somewhere causing mischief I'm sure. But you needn't worry about him; your safe now."

"What about Izzi. Is he here?"

"Good old Elsenplace," he said with a smile, "He's either here or there, up or down and sometimes in or out. Today he is out."

"Am I in Clown Alley?"

"Yes you are," he answered. "You have come far clown. You have reached the Great Center Ring, the very heart of Clown Alley for many generations. It has been a long and hard journey for the both of you. But even harder I think for Fiveish the Man, was it not?" he said with a wink.

"Somehow I don't think that the journey is over just yet," said Fiveish.

"No," said the Ringmaster, "It's just beginning."

Chapter Eighteen
The Beginning

FIVEISH JUST ADDED the finishing touches to his make-up by gluing the rubber clown nose to his face.

In the changing room next door the August Clown put the final piece of her costume on, the clown shoes.

They barged out of their doors at the same time, saw one another then broke out in laughter. They wrapped their arms around each other but stopped just short of hugging. They didn't want to smear their clown makeup, at least not yet.

He was decked out in a clown tux and she was attired in a clown wedding dress.

They walked hand in hand down a path towards the circus tent. They were each enjoying the crisp night air. As they went through the giant circus tent flap, a cheer went up from the crowd sitting in the bleachers and from all the circus entertainers.

In the middle of the center ring stood the Clown Alley archway with its strange and frightening faces and masks.

The cheering stopped then there was silence.

A calliope began playing "The Brides March" by Richard Wagner.

The Ringmaster stood to one side of the arch; the Stagehand stood to the other side.

The Tramp and the August stepped under the archway.

The Ringmaster adjusted his monocle then twisted his mustache. He had a devilishly playful smile.

"Do you Tramp Clown take this August Clown to be your Circus wife? To stick out your clown shoe and trip her? To knock her over the head with a rubber chicken? To have her crash through a base drum? To have and to hold when she does an Aerial Cartwheel? And to behave yourself and not cause too much pandemonium?"

"I do."

"Do you August Clown take this tramp to be your Circus husband? To chase him with a broom? To be his partner in shenanigans? To follow him through fiery hoops? To juggle razor sharp machete's with him? To have and to hold when he does an Arabian Dive Roll? And to behave yourself and not cause too much hullabaloo?

"I do."

The Ringmaster took off his top hat, tapped it several times then gave it a quick shake. Blue fog emanated from it; sparkling rays of light flashed into the sky.

"The bride may pull the Tramps nose."

August gently grabbed his clown nose then pulled him close. The nose did not come off.

"The groom may pull the August's nose."

The Tramp grabbed her clown nose and gave it a quick yank.

"Ouch!" she said.

"Oh, oh, I'm sorry."

The audience laughed out loud.

The two of them kissed. They tried to smear the makeup with their cheeks but their clown faces had magically become real clown faces.

They smiled then waved to the audience.

The calliope played "The Wedding March" by Felix Mendelssohn.

Suddenly, there was a powerful gust of wind. The top of the circus tent blew away into the darkness revealing the stars up above. The circus performers ran to their stations and then began performing their unique skills. But these were not just circus skills.

The high wire walkers floated in the air then sped in a circle around the tent perimeter.

The trapeze swingers flipped through the air then just kept on flipping and twisting, higher and higher until they were far above the circus.

The jugglers didn't just juggle balls, rings, and clubs; they juggled globes of light that lit up like stars and planets.

The human cannonball exploded out of his cannon. A trail of rainbow fire followed him through the night sky. He continued going up, up and up.

But the Ring Master had a golden aura surrounding him; a fiery ring of light that spun like a pinwheel with sparks spewing outward like the rotation of Andromeda.

The Tramp and the August looked at each other. Holding hands tightly, they jumped into the opening of the Ringmasters top hat, vanishing from sight.

RANCID SAT ALONE on a rickety stool in the middle of his filthy shack somewhere in No Mans Land. Rubbish was strewn all about. The walls were decorated with an eerie combination of surgical implements and magical props.

He rose from his seat then crawled onto his torn mattress.

Slipping headphones on, he clicked a small button on a hand held device. Resting his head on a grubby pillow, he quickly squashed a roach that attempted to skitter across it.

Beethoven's 7th Symphony the Allegretto, pumped into his head.

He pulled an old thread worn sweatshirt out from under his pillow; it had a faded picture of Beethoven on it. The image was hardly recognizable.

He brought the tattered shirt to his cheek. A tear fell from his eye; it dropped onto his pillow. Slowly, it was absorbed into the stained fabric then disappeared from sight.

About the Author

Frank Michael Adams grew up near
the beautiful beaches of Southern California.

He spent many years living by
the Vineyards of Sonoma County.

He currently resides at the foot of the Appalachia.

STEP RIGHT UP AND GET YOUR TICKETS
FOR THE NEXT EXCITING SHOW!

You Can Explore Clown Alley online at
www.clownalleybooks.com
Email: contact@clownalleybooks.com

Made in the USA
Middletown, DE
19 August 2022